EVOCATIONS

James Brogden is a part-time Australian who grew up in Tasmania and now lives with his wife and two daughters in Bromsgrove, Worcestershire, where he teaches English. His Midlands-based horror and fantasy stories have appeared in various anthologies and periodicals ranging from *The Big Issue* to *Dark Horizons* to the Award-Winning Alchemy Press anthologies. Snowbooks published his first novel, *The Narrows*, in 2012, followed by *Tourmaline* and its sequel *The Realt*, which appeared in May 2015.

Blogging occurs infrequently at

jamesbrogden.blogspot.co.uk

and tweeting at @skippybe.

EVOCATIONS

James Brogden

The Alchemy Press

The Alchemy Press, Staffordshire, UK

www.alchemypress.co.uk

Contents

Acknowledgements

'The Phantom Limb' © 2013. Originally published in *Den of Eek!*, 2013

'The Evoked' © 2011. Originally published in *Dark Horizons (BFS Journal)*, winter 2011

'The Last Dance of Humphrey Bear' © 2011. Originally published in *Dark Horizons (BFS Journal)*, summer 2011

'How to Get Ahead in Avatising' © 2014. Originally published in *The Alchemy Press Book of Urban Mythic 2*, 2014

'Junk Male' © 2014. Originally published in *Den of Eek: Urban Legends*, 2014

'The Decorative Water Feature of Nameless Dread' © 2013. Originally published in *Whispers From the Abyss*, 2013

'The Gestalt Princess' © 2012. Originally published in *Gears and Levers* (volume 1), 2012

'The Smith of Hockley' © 2013. Originally published in *The Alchemy Press Book of Urban Mythic 1*, 2013

'If Street' © 2012. Originally published in *The Alchemy Press Book of Ancient Wonders*, 2012

'Mob Rule' © 2015. Previously unpublished; new to this collection

'The Gas Street Octopus' © 2013. Originally published on the author's website; this is its first appearance in print

'DIYary of the Dead' © 2015. Originally published in *The Pun Book of Horror*, 2015

'The Curzon Street Horror' © 2013. Originally published in *Weird Trails*, 2013

'The Remover of Obstacles' © 2013. Originally published in *Urban Occult* , 2013

'Made From Locally Sourced Ingredients' © 2014. Originally published in *The Last Diner*, 2014

'The Pigeon Bride' © 2002. Originally published in *The Big Issue*, August 2002

Tourmaline (extract) © 2013. Originally published by Snowbooks, 2013

Dedication

To Peter, Jan, Jenny, Sarah, Theresa, Adrian, Colin, Kat, and Phyllis.

Thanks for letting me experiment on you.

Introduction

We first 'met' James Brogden back when we were editing *Dark Horizons* for The British Fantasy Society in 2011. He sent us 'The Last Dance of Humphrey Bear', a tale that melded horror and the macabre, which blew us away. Obviously we had to include it. When we asked for Christmas-themed stories for the winter issue, James responded with 'The Evoked', a splendidly chilling folk tale set both on a Sussex beach and in Heathrow Airport.

The Alchemy Press then embarked on a series of anthologies, and James came up trumps with three more superb stories that explored ancient myths and legends in a modern world: 'If Street', 'The Smith of Hockley' and 'How to Get Ahead in Avatising' – the type of stories we like. We mean, really, really like.

His love of myth and legend resurfaces with 'The Gestalt Princess' whilst 'The Decorative Water Feature of Nameless Dread' is a tongue-in-cheek nod to Cthulhu Mythos; more impish humour comes to the fore in 'Junk Male'. 'DIYary of the Dead' and 'The Last Dance of Humphrey Bear' are humorous in a far darker fashion, though no less enjoyable.

James also utilises familiar aspects of the world around him to reflect the darker edges of humanity. 'If Street' and

'The Smith of Hockley' as well as 'The Phantom Limb', 'The Gas Street Octopus', 'The Curzon Street Horror', 'The Remover of Obstacles' and 'The Pigeon Bride' are set in and around Birmingham; 'The Evoked' has an Australian theme to highlight the land where he spent most of his younger years.

James had his first novel published by Snowbooks: *The Narrows* appeared in 2012, followed by *Tourmaline* (2013) and the recently published *The Realt*. These novels confirm James' expertise at twisting and subverting the known world into the unknown.

Because The Alchemy Press was based in Birmingham (we're currently in the Staffordshire Moorlands) it was an obvious move to invite James along to one of our semi-regular Balti nights (Baltis – one of the major reasons to visit England's 'second' city), along with Joel Lane, Stan Nicholls, David Sutton et al. It was a good decision: James is an affable, gentle chap with a wicked sense of humour that infuses some of his stories (just read 'The Decorative Water Feature of Nameless Dread'). So, not only is he a brilliant writer, he is fantastic person and a rising star in the horror and fantasy firmaments. You've bought the book, now sit back and prepare to be heartily entertained. You have a treat in store.

Peter Coleborn / Jan Edwards
May 2015

The Phantom Limb

The doctors who amputated Alex's left arm below the elbow told him he would suffer phantom pains as the nerve endings in the stump tried to keep telling his brain that something was very wrong down there. They didn't tell him that he'd also be able to clench his non-existent fist and snap his non-existent fingers. And certainly no-one, least of all Alex, guessed that he might be able to touch anything in that place where the ghost of his dead arm still lived.

Or that anything there might reach out to touch him.

It had been a stupid accident. A weekend's narrow-boat holiday, for him and Kirsty to lazily meander through the heart of Birmingham's canal system, because at three miles an hour in a straight line, how hard could it be, right? Harder than it looked. The straight line became a zigzagging ricochet from bank to bank, and when they started heading towards another boat he panicked, tried to fend them off with a pole, slipped, and fifteen tons of steel-hulled narrow-boat lazily crushed everything below his elbow to the consistency of corned beef.

So off it came.

There was pain at first – but it became sporadic, and eventually nothing more than the occasional burst of pins and needles in his ghost flesh. There was talk of fitting him with a prosthesis, but when he found himself able to make a fist, and touch his fingers with his thumb, he decided against it. He couldn't move anything – at least not in the physical sense – but he could feel differences in temperature, wherever his hand was. Warm breezes. Sudden chills. He was convinced that somehow, somewhere, his hand was still working.

And then, one day, another hand grasped his.

It was sudden, the grip of someone in desperation. He freaked and pulled away with a yell. More carefully, as if reluctant to scare him away, the other hand returned, and with gentle, tentative touches convinced him that it meant no harm. It felt like a woman's hand – the fingers were slender, the skin smooth, the nails long and pointed. But her fingers quickly became agitated again, restlessly tapping a complex rhythm on his palm. She was trying to tell him something.

He taught himself the deaf-blind manual alphabet, which was basically sign-language by touch, and avoided mentioning anything about it to Kirsty, since there was something peculiarly intimate about communicating with another person purely by the sensation of their skin.

The first message came through: one simple word.

Help.

'Help how?' he asked. 'Who are you?'

Trapped, came the reply. *Please help. Pull.*

So he pulled with all the strength of his dead limb. Agonisingly, an inch of his lost fore-arm began to reappear. Then another inch. Then his hand. Then the hand that gripped his own.

And when he saw that it wasn't really a hand, and that the ravening creature it belonged to wasn't in the least bit like a woman, he began to scream.

The Evoked

When Australian gap-student Ricardo Preira receives a package from his Grannie in Sydney labelled 'Do Open Before Christmas', naturally he misreads this, and so he files it in the usual way by chucking it on top of the fridge which he shares with three other students in their Ealing flat. It joins a scree slope of junk mail which is slowly avalanching backwards into the Land of Dust Kittens.

It is an understandable mistake to make, and in any kind of fair world it wouldn't have cost anybody their life.

Three days later he will be scrabbling back through this pile with panicked, bloodstained fingers, sick with guilt but at the same time asking himself how could he possibly have known? For the moment, though, in the bright here and now, he tosses it without a second thought and goes back to turning the house upside down for his beach gear. Boardies, factor 20, Aussie flag towel, shades, cricket set.

It is 21st December – the midwinter solstice.

Patrick Turlowe is packing the back of his Discovery with the air of a man sleepwalking – not quite able to believe that he's actually let himself get talked into this – when Ricky phones.

'Hey wheelman,' Ricky shouts. Pat swears that the phone is actually bouncing in his hand. 'Where's these wheels, then?'

'You're serious about this, aren't you?'

'Shit no!' Ricky laughs. 'When am I ever serious about

anything? But we're still going to do it, if that's what you mean.'

'Ricky, mate, do you want to know what I'm doing right now?'

'Patrick.' Ricky's voice has taken on a note of warning. 'You're not naked, are you?'

'I'm chiselling the bloody ice off my car doors, that's what I'm doing! Have you got any idea what the temperature is outside?'

'Pat, I promised you a traditional Aussie Christmas on the beach, complete with sun, sand, and snags, if you are a very good boy. Your not turning up to drive makes you a bad boy, get it?'

He sighs. 'Got it.'

'Good. You're a legend. Seeyabit.' Ricky hangs up.

They pick up Jez, who is Ricky's bartending mate from the Eureka Stockade Bar in Camden, and Jez's new girlfriend Tanya, who has been invited at the very last minute and only after consultation with the others.

'This is exciting,' she says, clinging onto her bag in the back of Pat's Discovery. 'Are we off on some kind of magical mystery tour?'

The others look at her, then each other, and burst into laughter.

'What?' She is hurt, but very pretty even when she pouts (and certain parts of her anatomy are much poutier than others), suspicious of being the butt of someone's practical joke, looking to Jez for support.

Jez – who in his younger years looks a bit like a blond Roy Orbison – rallies. 'Hey, no, look guys, that's not fair. You told *me not to tell her anything.'* He appeals to her. *'They told me not to tell you.'*

'Tell me what?'

Ricky turns around and winks at her from the front seat. 'We're off to the seaside! Bags of lettuce and lashing of ginger beer, Timmy!'

And off they jolly well went.

*

Ricky woke with savage cramps in his neck and all down his left shoulder, and levered himself into a sitting position with a groan. Napping had been a mistake, airport departure lounge chairs not being famed for their orthopaedic design. There was a joke in that somewhere – he'd have a go at scribbling something down just as soon as his body unspasmed itself and he didn't feel quite so much like he'd just suffered a stroke.

He focussed blearily at the departures board. The red Delayed signs next to every flight number were unchanged, a solid vertical row like the world's shittest bingo game. Full house, he thought, and looked around at the other hundreds of passengers who were slumped in attitudes of weary resignation, heads on each other's shoulders or pillowed by rucksacks. The more energetic were shambling like zombies around the few duty-free and food outlets which were still open. *When there is no more room in hell the dead will walk the earth – and they shall seek out excellent deals on cheap Christmas flights with EasyJet.* Unbelievably, the airport Tannoy was playing Wham's 'Last Christmas'. It was half-past ten in the evening.

He'd been here for eight hours.

With disgust, he realised that the side of his face was sticky with sleep-drool, so he took his flight bag and went in search of the loos.

Overhead fluorescents should be banned, he decided. They shone straight through his thinning hair as if it wasn't there at all and put big dark circles under his eyes. Christ he looked old. He splashed some water on his face, brushed his teeth, and was trying to straighten out some of the worst wrinkles in his jacket when he noticed that the man at the next sink was trying not to look at him in that peculiarly intense way which meant he'd been half-recognised. The guy looked about as raddled as Ricky himself, and so probably wasn't sure that he was seeing who he thought he was seeing; soon he'd go away and find his mates, and they'd cluster together at a safe distance where a whispered conversation would take place along the lines of, 'It is him', 'No it bloody isn't', 'Of course it is. Go and ask him', 'I'm not bloody asking him, you bloody ask him'. But he couldn't say anything, because how arrogant would it be to smile smugly and say, 'Hi. Yes, it's me. It's Ricky Preira, B-list stand-up and raconteur', if the guy wasn't a fan and didn't give a toss? So he did his best to not look so much like a scutter and went back out to stretch his legs in the departures lounge from which nobody was departing.

He stopped for a moment by one of the big windows overlooking the runway and watched snow swirling heavily in the floodlit darkness. Orange-strobing snowploughs were slogging up and down the tarmac while maintenance crews in hi-vis jackets sprayed gallons of de-icer over planes which were covered again in a matter of minutes. The snow had come much faster and thicker than predicted, and scenes of similarly chaotic conditions around the country were looping on the rolling news channels. Thousands of travellers heading abroad for the festive season were delayed, some of them for days. Silver lining, though – at least he wasn't one of the poor sods trapped on the snowbound motorways.

In the black-mirror reflection of the lounge super-imposed on this scene, he noticed the jolly face of a shop-front cardboard Father Christmas.

'Don't think I don't know what you're up to,' he told it. 'It won't work.'

He made a slow lap of the lounge, wondering as ever what the hell it was with airports and Toblerone, and failing to avoid looking for his DVD in the WH Smith. 'Do not look for your own product on the shelves', his agent Stephanie had said. 'You'll either find it and get depressed because nobody's bought it, or not find it, which is worse.' There were no copies. Ricky knew he shouldn't be surprised that a retail outlet the same size as a shower cubicle didn't stock the DVD of his not-quite-sell-out performance which had toured some of the UK's most prestigious middle-sized arts centres and working men's clubs and been met with a resounding critical 'meh' from the entertainment press. *Please Do Not Feed the Paranoia*, it was called. How very fucking apt.

Once he saw an old bearded man asleep in a seat, and his heart lurched in terror, but then he saw that it was just another delayed traveller.

Three quarters of the way around his lap – by now with a coffee (but not the limited edition seasonal gingerbread-flavoured one, because you never could be too careful where that kind of thing would lead) – he saw the guy from the loo again, sitting with a large group of friends and family. Three small kids were looking tired and grizzly. Ricky had never wanted children himself, but he felt sorry for the parents all the same. The guy looked up, made eye contact. Ricky tipped his coffee in recognition. Yep, you got it.

The guy came over. He was thirty-ish, crop-haired, all trainers and Aston Villa strip. Dressed for somewhere a lot warmer than here. Completely normal. 'Um,' he said, 'sorry mate, this is going to sound really stupid, but are you Ricky Preira?'

'I could deny it,' Ricky replied, 'but then I'd have to kill you.'

'Sweet!' the guy laughed. 'I don't mean to bother you, but we was just wondering, you know.'

'I know. It's cool.'

'We loved you in that *Mock the Week* special. Is it true what they say about those Christmas specials being filmed in the middle of summer?'

'Some of them, probably. We did that one in October.'

'Doesn't it ruin the Christmas spirit a bit?'

'The Christmas Spirit is more than capable of looking

after itself, trust me. Anyway, I'm glad you enjoyed it.'

'Cheers. Have a Merry one, yeah?'

Don't say it. Never say it. 'You too.' The man went back to his family, where there was much excited whispering, and Ricky went back to his seat, and remembered.

*

Dank grey slabs of Sussex farmland slide past outside the windows, drizzle-smudged and indistinct. Such dourness is expected of the city and suburbs, but somehow he has been expecting the English countryside to be a bit brighter and less, well, bloody miserable-looking, to be honest.

'All I'm saying,' says Pat to Ricky, 'is that your track record with this sort of thing isn't exactly spotless, that's all. Remember Easter? Rabbits everywhere. It was like that episode from Father Ted.*'*

'Which one?' asks Tanya.

Pat looks at her. 'The one with all the rabbits?'

'Oh!' Tanya brightens, that mystery having been solved.

Pat shakes his head. 'Then there was your eighteenth,' he continues.

'What happened then?' She is intrigued.

'Fancy dress. Brilliant party. Everything sweet as, until come midnight and suddenly everybody believes that they are actually what they've come dressed as. Total carnage. We had three ambulances at one point.'

'Oh it wasn't so bad,' Ricky protests.

'Easy for you to say,' Jez huffs. 'You didn't go dressed as Priscilla Queen of the Fucking Desert.'

'You pulled, didn't you?'

Tanya has been thinking hard about this. 'What about

Hallowe'en?' she asks.

'We don't talk about Hallowe'en,' Ricky says darkly. 'Ever.'

An uneasy silence fills the car as they drive south.

Jukes Cove has been scooped from the chalk of Sussex's Jurassic coastline over tens of millennia by a peculiar combination of tides such that it is impossible to see until you are almost on top of it – and that is only made possible by a fiddly B-road which switchbacks down through a series of blind turns. Pat babies his four-wheel drive down here, squinting through the windscreen. His satnav has long since given up, and insists that they are currently five-hundred yards offshore. A sketch-work of winter-bare trees nets the grey sky and hawthorn fingers scrabble at the vehicle's sides.

Tanks had once grumbled along the coast during World War Two, and there are still a few crumbling pillboxes owned by the National Trust, which are visited by tenacious bunker-junkies hiking along the windswept cliff paths.

The road levels out and dead-ends at a pot-holed car park with a locked ticket booth and a rusted barrier bearing a sign which tells them that the 'resort' is closed Out of Season. Pat simply parks in front of it. Not exactly holding up a massive queue of eager holidaymakers. Further, waves toy half-heartedly with a pebbled shoreline.

Jez looks at the place and sings 'Oh I do love to be beside the seaside,' in a cynical undertone.

'Um, is this it?' Tanya wraps her cardie tightly about her shoulders and shivers.

'Misery guts, the lot of ya,' Ricky chides them, and bounces out. His flip-flops crunch gravel down to the funless sea. This place will do nicely. When he realises that nobody is following him, he turns back. *'Well come on then! You don't think I can do this on my own, do you?'*

'Well, yeah,' says Pat. *'That's sort of what we're expecting.'*

'It's a party,' Ricky explains. *'A party needs people. You can't call the spirit of the occasion without people to make the occasion. So out, you bunch of gutless wonders. Now.'*

They follow him down to the beach, where Ricky makes them stand in a loose circle holding hands. All except Tanya.

'Why not me too?'

'This is an Aussie Christmas,' Ricky reminds her. *'You get dual nationality all of a sudden?'*

Tanya grumps.

'Look,' Ricky softens. *'It's nothing personal. You'll see. Go slap on some factor fifty and enjoy the show. Right then, my little ex-pat dahlings,'* he said to the other two, *'close your eyes.'*

'You what?'

'Fucksake, Jez!'

'Fine.' He closes them.

'Now, everybody nice and homesick? Cool. Tell me what you remember about Christmas at home. I'll go first. Nights so hot you can barely sleep, maybe just under a single sheet, if that.' He waited. *'Come on then!'*

Pat shrugs, says, 'Barbecues.'

'Obviously, duh. Be specific.'

'Okay, uh, burnt sausages. Lamb chops.'

'Pavlova,' says Jez.

'Eucalyptus and pine sap, smelling all dusty.'

'This is so gay,' mutters Tanya.

But the momentum has caught.

'The Sydney-Hobart yacht race on Boxing Day.'

'Calamine lotion all over your mozzie bites.'

'Cold beer!'

'Is it me or is it getting warmer?'

'Shut up!' Ricky snaps. 'Keep going! You know what I mean.'

He feels their shared reminiscence flowing into him through their linked hands and building up behind his breastbone, filling up something which feels like a third lung, so he opens his mouth and it streams out silently in something which feels like a call. In a way this is easier than a birthday because Christmas is so big that people's connections to it are much stronger. On the other hand, there are so few of them present that he doesn't know if their combined call will be loud enough.

For moment the universe hangs, undecided.

Damn, but if it isn't actually getting hotter.

They all hear Tanya gasp in astonishment at the same time as a suddenly much bigger wave crashes over their feet – not at all the freezing cold of the English Channel – and they open their eyes.

Blisteringly hot sun hammers out of a sky so blue you can sharpen a knife on it. The pebble shoreline is now a scalloped crescent of honey-coloured sand against which the tourmaline-green sea dashes itself in foaming breakers. Jukes Cove is still the same dimensions as before, and they can see that the encompassing headlands on either side still brood under the grey gloom of a British midwinter. But down here ... oh, down here...

Ricky gives a great whoop and sprints for the sea, shucking clothes and plunging into the surf. After a moment's hesitation the others follow.

It is quite some time before any of them notice the bearded old man glaring down at them from the cliffs.

*

Ricky sat and tried to write some jokes about airport zombies, but without much success. In all honesty, he wasn't actually that talented a writer. He had stage presence, sure, had always been the life and soul of the party, but that and the success which had followed over the years had all stemmed from his peculiar ability to call out the spirit of any given gathering of people. He'd learned early on that he could hold the attention of crowds with even the most banal of performances, and by a combination of luck and outright blaggery had somehow managed to turn it into a career. To begin with he'd thought himself unusual, but after his first few brushes with middling fame he strongly suspected that it was a talent which quite a few celebrities shared. Still, he'd never known anybody else who was able to change things with it.

Evocatori, his Grannie had called them, in the letter that he'd read too late. *Those who call forth.* The priests and shamen of the ancient world, now the stand-up comedians and politicians of the modern, not communing with the gods but creating them out of the consensual gestalt of the mob mind – drawing them out, giving them life and form.

At each one of his gigs – if they were going well – Ricky would see, sitting right in the front row, a figure who hadn't been there before no matter how packed it might have been. Sometimes male, sometimes female – always laughing the loudest at his jokes and always first to call for an encore. Evoked from the crowd. Once he'd seen that, he'd started looking for the Evoked at other events: concerts, riots, even traffic jams. At a particularly nasty Arsenal/Chelsea grudge match he'd seen their respective mascots – Gunnersaurus Rex and Big Lupus – hacking the bejeezus out of each other on the sidelines, though later the men who normally wore the suits claimed to have been having a fag-break together at the time. The Evoked were always where the numbers of people were thickest, and where emotions ran high.

It might be interesting to see what he could call out of hundreds of stranded airport passengers, but he had a suspicion that it might be rather depressing. Plus, the mob was notoriously unpredictable; there was a very real danger of summoning up the Christmas spirit by accident.

He became aware that Villa Dad was hovering nearby again in the twitchy manner of someone plucking up courage to ask for an autograph. He switched on his smile and looked up.

'What can I help you with?'

'This is going to sound really cheeky, but there's a bunch of families who have got ourselves together, mostly for the kids, and we were planning on doing something Christmassy, you know, to keep them occupied, and we were just wondering if maybe, you know, you'd join in?'

'Do a Cliff Richard Wimbledon job, you mean? Blitz

spirit and all that.'

The man laughed nervously. 'Yeah, sort of.'

Ricky sighed. He should have known this was coming. 'I hate to be a killjoy, but it's really not my kind of thing.' The man reddened with embarrassment and actually stumbled back a step as if Ricky had just slapped him. 'Hey, no, fine, it's cool. Sorry to bother you again.' He went back to the group of families, and Ricky could see them talking it over in hushed tones. One or two dirty glances came his way from the mothers.

'Shit.'

*

From the back of Pat's car come beach blankets, a sun umbrella, Christmas crackers, cold barbecued chicken and a dozen different kinds of salad, beer, and soft drinks for the Designated Driver. Ricky and his friends swim, eat, play crap beach cricket wearing their cracker crowns, swim again and then eat some more before collapsing in the sun.

It is while they are debating the viability of a second innings that Ricky notices the old man staring at them from the western headland.

'Scary old fart, three o'clock,' he says, pointing. It is hard to make out details against the blazing late afternoon sun, but the man seems to be bearded, dressed in hiking clothes and a red woollen beanie. A rucksack bulges behind him.

'Bunker junkie,' says Jez dismissively, reaching for another mince pie. 'Because how much fun is it poking around in old dead shit.'

'A more interesting question is what does he see when he looks down here? Does he see us lolling around in the sun or

freezing our nads off?'

'Who cares?' yawns Tanya. 'We're not hurting anyone. Let him look.' She is stretched out in her bikini and looks completely fantastic. 'Right', she says, climbing languorously to her feet in a way which is impossible for the boys to ignore. 'One last swim, I think.' And she trots off down to the water.

Only Ricky continues to pay any attention to the old man on the headland. He isn't hiking, and doesn't appear to be interested in looking for old bunkers. He is definitely watching Ricky and his friends. Old perv. It makes his skin crawl. He gets up, brushes himself down, and heads for the car to get some clothes on. Once there, he looks back and sees that the old man's stance has shifted fractionally. His head has turned.

He is just watching Ricky.

As if realising that he's been rumbled, the old man turns away, raises one outstretched hand to the sky, and makes a grabbing gesture as if clawing something back from thin air.

And the sun disappears.

In its place appear slate-coloured clouds. The sand becomes stone, and the temperature crashes – not just rapidly, but instantaneously.

Twenty yards offshore, the effect on Tanya is as if she has been dropped into the middle of the Arctic Ocean. Sudden shock causes her to gasp a huge lungful of air and start hyperventilating, making it impossible to shout for help. Her scream of 'Jez!' comes out as an asthmatic 'Jehhhhhhh... Jehhhhhh...' before dizziness and flaring black spots before her eyes stop her from seeing or saying anything at all. Then her limbs lock in spasm and a freezing swell rolls over her head but she is still gasping, except now her lungs are full with a crushing ice-burning weight of water and one of those black spots is getting bigger and bigger and bigger and...

*

The day after Tanya's funeral it is Christmas Eve and Ricky is getting paid double time at the Eureka Stockade Bar. He doesn't want to be here, but Jez has understandably gone home and it's Ricky's first time in London, which is a bloody expensive place to live and he can do with every penny he gets. The bar is heaving. There are enough of the regulars in who know what happened and buy him drinks in commiseration, so that by the time midnight rolls around he's drinking more than he's serving, but Doug the head barman cuts him some slack too. The air is warm and golden, all polished wood and brass. He sings along with the standard seasonal pop songs on the juke box, and even gets a snog off a pretty girl. Christmas in winter is a million miles away from what he's been used to as a child, but at the same time instantly familiar. He loves everybody in the room.

He doesn't see the old man in the red beanie and rucksack until it is too late.

The Evoked is standing in the middle of the room while people dance and drink and reel obliviously around him. He should be jolly given the crowd that he has been called from, but for some reason he looks mightily pissed off.

When he sees Ricky looking, he makes that clawing motion at the air again – grabbing something back. Recalling it.

And the first fight breaks out.

It starts with arguments: drunken tears, accusations, recriminations. A face is slapped. Friends stand up for each other in little tribes, squaring off against other tribes. Yelling.

Doug sees what's coming but is hopelessly outnumbered. Eventually there is smashed glass, screaming, and the heavy thunder-rain patter of blood. And not just in one place: it is happening all over the room.

Ricky lunges through the chaos towards the old man. 'Stop this!' he yells. 'What are you doing? What do you want?'

The old man leans in close. His breath smells of stale gingerbread and there are lice crawling in his beard. 'I should ask you the same thing, Evocatore.' He spits the last word venomously. 'What do you want from me? Do you even know?' For a moment he seems to be searching for something in Ricky's face, but then snorts with contempt. 'No. I'll not be enslaved to a spoilt, witless child like you.'

Then somebody's fist connects with Ricky's head and the old man is gone.

In the early hours of Christmas morning, when he returns to his flat stitched and bandaged and bloodied, he scrabbles for the parcel from his Grannie – the letter which he should have read days ago – and starts to learn what he is.

*

Ricky saw that some of the graveyard-shift airport staff had acquired a Father Christmas costume and were doing the rounds of the departure lounge singing carols and handing out sweets. A swarm of small children surrounded them as they headed, Pied-Piper-style, in his direction, so he decided the safest thing to do was to keep out of everybody's way by going to play on the concourse travellators.

The airport muzak system was now playing Wizzard's 'I Wish it Could be Christmas Every Day.' *No you don't*, he thought. *You wouldn't, not if you could see what it can do.*

He was practising the fine art of going nowhere fast by walking the wrong way along one of the travellators, maintaining position by his reflection in the black-mirror window, when his phone bongled to let him know that he had a text from Stephanie.

Wot dfuk u up2? Chek twitr!

It seemed that his agent was not pleased.

He did as directed and checked his Twitter feed, discovering with mounting horror that some of the other delayed passengers were tweeting about him being a selfish sod who wouldn't join in a simple sing-song – accompanied by pictures of him looking grumpy and hacked off, taken with somebody's phone. The whisperers. Don't feed the paranoia? Why bother – it was completely self-sustaining.

His phone bongled again: *PR nitemare! Kiss NY goodbye. Play nicely, Scrooge!*

He replied *OK mum* and let the travellators take him back to where he belonged, racking his brains for a way out of this. How did you keep an audience entertained at Christmas without evoking the Christmas spirit? He wasn't a writer – he couldn't make up anything new. An answer came to him then, and it was so cheeky that he simply couldn't resist.

There was a definite frostiness in the departure lounge as he returned, but when he turned on the trademark grin, clapped his hands together and said, 'Right then, who's for a good old-fashioned Christmas ghost story?'

the smiles returned, and he began to feel like he was in control for the first time since the initial 'delayed' sign had appeared. Outside, the snow still threw itself at the windows in fury, but here it was warm, with people huddled in nests of airport blankets, and he felt the familiar sensation of being taken to the audience's heart.

Careful now. Peace on earth and goodwill to all men is not the goal here. Fear is. Evoke something small and terrified which won't be a threat to anybody.

So he told them what he'd learned the day after coming back from the hospital.

'This is the story of the very first Christmas in July. Unless you're Australian you probably won't have heard about it, but basically it's the idea that since Christmas in the southern hemisphere falls in the middle of summer, some people like to celebrate a midwinter Christmas in July. They go up into the mountains where they build snowmen, sing carols and pull crackers, while here we're watching Wimbledon and mowing our lawns.

'People believe that it's a very recent idea – that it's only been going for fifty years or so – but I'm going to tell you the story about the first one which happened a lot earlier than that. It went terribly wrong – so wrong that nobody dared have another for a hundred years.'

He waited for the oohs and ahhs.

'In 1842 a settler called John Barker arrived in New South Wales with his family and over the next twenty years established himself in the Snowy Mountains as a very rich and successful grazier and stockman, with no regrets about leaving England. However, his wife, Charlotte, felt very differently about things, and she never conquered her homesickness for the green fields of Lancashire. Two times of the year were especially bad for her: Christmas, when she most missed her family on the other side of the world, and in July, when the higher peaks of the Snowies turned as white as the Alps.

'And so one year she had a brilliant idea – to combine the two – and John, being the good and loving husband that he was, did everything in his means to furnish her with this dream. He bought land and built a house in a high, remote area called the Perisher Valley, and when it was complete he arranged for their entire household to be moved there for two weeks whilst they celebrated an unseasonal yuletide.

'They took everything with them. They had a turkey supper and a Christmas tree with presents underneath it for the children. They sang carols and made snowmen, and had even brought a parson with them to deliver a proper service of nine lessons.

'This was their mistake.

'The parson, unknown to himself, was a descendant of the ancient Roman Evocatores – the war priests who would call forth the spirit of Mars to fill the legionnaire's hearts with fiery blood, and who, when an enemy city fell, would enslave that city's god to the service of Rome. This lineage is what made him such a good parson – in the right and proper circumstances he could evoke the Holy Spirit from his congregation and bring them closer to God

– but it's also what spelled death for everybody in that house.

'He should have read his own Bible more closely. Ecclesiastes says "To everything there is a season", and it applies just as much to Christmas as anything else. Christmas hibernates during the rest of the year, like a bear. I'm sure you know how dangerous it can be to disturb one of those. He evoked the Christmas spirit with spectacular success, probably because of Charlotte's ardent desire for it and the household's great excitement, but Christmas was confused. This was not when and where he was meant to be. What were these people doing here, in the middle of summer, waking him up? He was disorientated, angry, and lashed out violently to restore the equilibrium which had been disturbed.

'The fire was visible for miles. Of course, there was nothing resembling a fire brigade and no hope whatsoever of rescue. When people finally arrived and started sifting through the ashes, it was thought that a stray spark from the open fire must have set the Christmas tree alight. The bodies of John Barker, his wife Charlotte, their children, and all of their servants were so badly burned as to be unrecognisable. Some say that they had also suffered appalling injuries, as if something huge had attacked and killed them before the fire, but no doctor ever saw the bodies, and so nothing can ever be proven.

'One thing I do know for sure – and that is the parson's name. He was a Dutch immigrant, and his name was Joseph Preira.

'He was my great-great-grandfather.'

The hoped-for gasp didn't materialise, and for a moment Ricky thought he'd mistimed the punch-line.

Then the passenger – the extra passenger, the one who hadn't been in the room when the story had started, the one sitting right in the middle of everybody – got up. He was old, bearded, wearing a red beanie on his head and a battered rucksack on his back.

'We know,' he said. His voice was low, and trembling with rage.

Ricky's legs turned traitor, unhinging and dropping him backwards in his seat. He couldn't speak, couldn't think. He was so stunned that he wasn't sure he could even see the man properly. 'You…' he managed. 'But…'

'What's more Christmassy than a good old fashioned ghost story?' asked the man, stepping forward through the audience. They sat as still as any congregation, their eyes fixed on Ricky. 'Well, I'll tell you. It all depends on what sort of Christmas you're talking about. Take me, for example. I'm older than both your modern Coca Cola Santa and that bastardised version of Saint Nicholas, never mind the Christ child. I'm what it all boils down to. I'm your fear that one day the dark will come and never leave, and I've been around since you were gibbering in caves at midwinter and killing each other's children to bring the sun back.

'I am Yule.

'And you presume to order me? Do you want a winter Christmas in the middle of summer or a summer

Christmas in the middle of winter? Do you want to worship the cornerstone of your faith or just have lots of shiny new toys to play with and a chance to shag each other at the office party? Well? Which is it? I asked you once before what it was you wanted from me. Do you have an answer yet?'

Ricky was paralysed and speechless with terror.

Yule was standing over him now, stinking of blood and gingerbread. He snorted with contempt. 'I thought not. You don't deserve the birthright of your forefathers. I will do this one last thing for you, however. I will perform the function for which you evoked me: I will make the sacrifice which turns the dark away.'

He made that grabbing action one final time – clawing through Ricky's flesh, then muscle and sinew, and finally past the flat plate of his breastbone to his juddering heart, and he took it back.

He took it all back.

The last thing that Ricky's dying eyes saw, as they wandered up from the wet, splintered wreckage of his own torso, was that it had finally stopped snowing outside.

The Last Dance of Humphrey Bear

Simon Smith watched the young family enter Accident and Emergency and hugged Humphrey Bear close with his good arm to stop the toy from squirming so hungrily that people noticed.

Even Nurse Timms, who was as wonderfully normal as any human soul had a right to be, saw something odd about them and paused in the process of bandaging up his bad arm.

The family looked like television images badly superimposed upon each other, and where they overlapped at the edges they burned – the daughter most of all. He made Humphrey Bear do a little dance for her, one-handed, as she was carried past in her mother's arms; the movement caught her attention and she smiled wanly, giving a little wave in return. Her fingers fizzed and trailed fire like the after-images of Bonfire Night sparklers. After a decade on the streets Simon Smith had often seen that in the onionskin layers of reality, those closest to death flamed uppermost.

The little girl was ablaze.

The father – or at least, the rat-faced young man who followed them – hesitated as they passed through the sliding glass doors, checking out the waiting area.

Social workers, Simon Smith knew. He was checking to see if there were any social workers in here. Or policemen.

'Listen, Simon,' said Nurse Timms distractedly, watching the family approach Reception, 'do you think you can hang on here for just a bit?'

Humphrey Bear nodded his head. *No problem.*

'Good, that's great. I'll come back as soon as I can.' She packed away the dressing kit and the filthy old bandages for incineration. Simon Smith wasn't his real name, of course, but it had been nice of her to make one up for him.

Afterwards, Nurse Timms told the police that the first signs she'd noticed that anything might be wrong was when she'd examined the child, but the truth was that she knew the girl was going to die when she saw that little wave. It was a joyless gesture of farewell rather than greeting – the way a condemned prisoner might say goodbye to their loved ones on the way to the gas chamber. She wasn't aware of the knowledge, however. It bypassed the front of her brain completely and slithered straight down her spine, raising goose-bumps all the way, until it came to rest, coiled like ice in her stomach.

She was so preoccupied that she didn't notice when Simon Smith slipped a pair of shining scissors from her dressing kit into his sleeve.

*

At the front desk the mother – pallid and tired, the only

colour in her face the bruised circles of fatigue under her eyes – was explaining that her little girl had hurt her arm falling out of bed, while the boyfriend (no wedding ring, Nurse Timms noted) hovered nearby, scowling.

'Hallo there, princess,' she said to the girl. 'What's your name then?'

'Sianne,' mother replied. 'She's six.'

Sianne. Pronounced *sigh-anne*. Mother had probably seen the name in a copy of *Heat* magazine and thought that was how it sounded, then forgotten how to spell it on the birth certificate. If there was one. Sianne, wrapped in a blanket, was large-eyed and shivering, a combination of cold and shock.

'How did you hurt your arm?'

'She fell out of bed,' the boyfriend interrupted from immediately behind them. His breath stank of cigarettes. 'Whacked it on the edge, silly sod. Just strap her up, alright? And we'll go.'

As if embarrassed at how readily this answer came, mother added: 'She sleeps on the top bunk. I think she must have caught her arm under the safety bar thing and twisted it when she fell.'

She fell out of bed.

She sleep-walked down the stairs.

She crawled under the kitchen table and pulled a chair over onto herself.

Variations on a theme.

'Sure, let's have a look at that, then, shall we?'

Nurse Timms unwrapped the blanket slightly from

around the girl's forearm and peeked inside. She'd been expecting something minor like a graze, some bruising, possibly even a cut which had been too big for mother's sticking plasters. They'd end up having to wait a couple of hours, which was a pain, but kids were tough. They bounced. She'd most likely drop off again in mother's lap.

It was a credit to Nurse Timms' professionalism that her smile hardly faltered at all when she saw the actual state of Sianne's lower arm. The only way the girl could have done this by falling out of the top bunk was if her bed had been halfway up a mountain.

'Right!' she said brightly, 'we'll find you a cubicle and get a doctor to have a look at you straight away, okay?'

*

Simon Smith watched the girl being wheel-chaired away. He knew well enough what would be happening, and so was content to wait.

The doctors would want to take x-rays of the girl's other limbs too. Just a precaution, they would assure mother, normal procedure in cases like these, in case Sianne had hurt anything else; they hoped mother would understand. Simon Smith thought that she might understand all too well. She could hardly object. It might even be why she'd brought her daughter to a hospital, though not consciously.

That was when they'd find the old fractures – the ones which had healed crookedly on their own. The ones going back to when the girl had been a baby.

When the young man came stalking back through the

waiting area with a face like thunder and returned an hour later to drop off an overnight bag Simon Smith knew that the girl and her mother had been moved upstairs to the paediatric ward. He watched a number of importantly -suited doctors and officials hurry to and fro, heads together, talking in low, urgent tones: the radiologist, the paediatric registrar, the Social Services duty officer. He knew them well by sight after all the other times he had watched and waited here, though he doubted they were even aware of his existence. Sometimes the invisibility of homelessness was a blessing. It couldn't be relied on, though. He would still have to be careful. It was just a matter of waiting until the evening got busy, between when the pubs closed and the nightclubs chucked out.

Taking inventory was a good way to kill time. Eighteen strip-lights. Forty-six orange plastic chairs. Thirty-seven patients watching the scrolling red-LED notice board. Six self-inflicted cuts on the inside of his left fore-arm, one for every day of the week so far. When it got to seven he would add one to his right arm. He already had five there. When that got to seven too he would transfer all forty-nine days to his chest with the burning end of a cigarette. Currently the tally was sixteen burn-scars over his heart – which, including both daily and weekly arms, totalled eight hundred and twenty five days since his Jenny had died, or a little over two years.

Three stitches left across Humphrey Bear's mouth. A little over two years ago he'd sewn a line of big clumsy crosses with thick rainbow-coloured thread, and so far he'd used six – some on children like Sianne, but some just because he'd been lonely.

Eventually the drunks invaded, bleeding and vomiting and fighting, and in the chaos it was a simple matter to walk unnoticed to the lifts that led to the children's ward.

*

The corridors upstairs were dim and quiet, a sleeping labyrinth of distant murmurs. The ward door – despite being covered in bright cartoon pictures of bandaged Disney characters – was heavy and key-code locked, with a pane of reinforced glass so that the duty nurse far down the corridor on the other side could see to admit only parents and other hospital staff.

The thing about a heavy, slow-swinging door, Simon Smith knew, was that people rarely ever checked to make sure that it had closed properly – and they absolutely never looked to see if anybody else had slipped in silently behind them.

He eased his way carefully between the curtains which separated one cubicle from another, past the children who slept there. Bandaged, hooked up to drips and machines – still they seemed enviably peaceful. If there was any consolation to be had here, it was that they were the victims of nature's cruelty rather than their loved ones'.

He found Sianne. The little girl was fast asleep with her good arm clutching a filthy blanket embroidered with cartoon letters of the alphabet. Her mouth was open; 'catching flies', they'd called it when Jenny had slept in just that way. Of course, Jenny never had her whole other arm encased in a bright pink fibreglass cast. She'd have loved the colour.

Sianne's mother was asleep on a narrow foldaway camping cot low down next to the hospital bed. With both asleep the resemblance between them was so striking that for a moment he almost felt some sympathy for the mother.

It passed quickly.

He brought out the scissors.

He paused for a moment, wondering if Nurse Timms would get in trouble for this later.

With breathless care, he slipped the pointed lower jaw of the scissors beneath one of the last three crosses stitched across Humphrey Bear's mouth, and cut. It resisted, tougher than a simple twist of frayed wool had any right to be, before it finally parted with a grisly snip like an umbilical cord.

The toy's chest heaved once, deeply, and expelled a sudden rush of breath. It flowed over and past him in a wave which smelled both dry and sweet, something like cinnamon and strawberries, or old toothpaste and cotton pyjamas; a child's sleep-smell. It robbed him of sight and plunged him into another place; a darkness which hovered in his peripheral vision, brimming behind his eyes:

Afterwards – once he has calmed down and cleaned up the broken glass and spilled wine – he goes upstairs to check on Jenny.

Her nightlight is on, and the nursery school mobile of

colourful fishes swims lazily in a breeze from the window. He can see the dim shape of her body, tiny in the new big bed now that she has graduated from her cot. He hasn't realised how tense he is until he hears her light breathing, and expels a huge relieved sigh of his own.

He can't have shaken her all that hard.

Then he sees the open, staring eyes and his heart stops.

Somehow he is across the room, swimming through the air, batting aside the fishes, reaching down for her – and sees that it is just her BearBuddy Humphrey. The one that she chose himself, named in the shop, stuffed and brushed and placed a small embroidered heart inside along with a whispered wish that not even Mummy or Daddy heard. Humphrey is nestled in the crook of Jenny's neck, dressed in his best BearBuddy pyjamas, with his friendly plastic eyes gleaming in the nightlight's amber glow.

It's okay, Jenny is just asleep. Her right arm is draped lovingly across the bear's fluffy tummy, pale except for where the bruises have started to darken, rising and falling gently with the motion of its ... its...

Breathing.

Humphrey is breathing.

And when he looks closer he sees that Jenny isn't. There is also something very wrong about the crook of her neck into which Humphrey is so comfortably cuddled.

He stares, uncomprehending, between his daughter and the bear – one seeming to be so peacefully asleep, the other impossibly alive, and then he begins to scream.

He is always screaming.

For a moment the onslaught of memory was so strong

that he couldn't tell whether the girl in the bed was now, in front of him, or in the past. Then he came to and quickly placed the bear close by the mother's face before his dead daughter's breath dissipated into the air and was lost.

She inhaled deeply and stirred in her sleep, as if aware on some level that something was trying to enter her. Then she woke up.

She saw him crouched down by her pillow and smiled sleepily. 'Hello Daddy,' she murmured.

'Hello baby,' he whispered through sudden tears.

'I'm tired.'

'I know, baby, I know. Not long now.'

'Can I sleep now?'

'Soon,' he promised. He stroked a stray wisp of hair that wasn't his daughter's away from the face that wasn't his daughter's face. It still smelled like her, but that was fading quickly. There wasn't much time. So much he wanted to say, but couldn't. 'Baby, can you do something for me?'

'Yes, Daddy. What?'

'There's a girl. Her name is Sianne. Do you know her?'

The woman's face frowned in childlike concentration. 'Ye-es,' she said slowly. 'I think so.' She seemed confused. 'Do I have … is she my sister? I can't remember.'

'It's okay. She's a friend.'

'She's sad. Her arm hurts. The man hurt her.'

'I know, baby, I know.'

'Is she going to die like the others?'

He wanted to say of course not, or that he hoped she wouldn't, but the lies wouldn't come. 'Can you tell me where she lives?' he asked. Anything the mother knew, Jenny – or what there was of Jenny inside her – would also know.

Jenny told him.

Before he had a chance to say goodbye, she was gone, and there were only two rainbow stitches left.

Sianne was awake and staring at him with wide eyes.

Simon Smith froze in panic, but Humphrey Bear came to his rescue, dancing a comical little can-can along the safety rail of her bed, and she smiled. Simon Smith placed a finger to his lips: *shh*. She echoed the gesture.

Shh…

As carefully as his hammering heart would allow, he crept from the children's ward, trailed all the way by her silent, watchful eyes.

*

How much had she seen? He would give anything to be able to ask, but that was impossible. The rules laid down by the Nuthers were intractable and unforgiving.

'Nuthers' had been Jenny's word for anybody outside her immediate family: doctors, delivery men, people in shops. Strangers. It suited well enough for his purposes.

They'd come to him that first night as he sat cradling her body, paralysed with the horror of what he had done and waiting for the ambulance. Three indistinct figures watching him coldly from the shadowed corners of her bedroom. They'd told him the secrets of how he could bring her back, tossed him the spool of rainbow thread and the golden needle with which he'd sewn up Humphrey Bear's mouth, and added that as a further penance he would speak no longer to any living soul or hers would be forfeit.

He suspected that he had simply gone insane – that was the conclusion which the courts had drawn – but if that were the case he couldn't see the virtue in sanity. Once, just once, he'd tried to explain the Nuthers to a prison psychiatrist. As punishment for that transgression the Nuthers had taken one of Humphrey's stitches and added a vow of self-chastisement to his one of silence.

He found an alley behind the hospital crowded with overflowing dumpsters, and addressed the darkness.

'I know you're there. I want to ask for something.'

He waited. They didn't always come when he asked, either because they were off on whatever business they had of their own, or simply taunting him with their non-existence.

Then the Nuthers were in the alley with him. His imagination, desperate to hook something recognisable onto the unreality of what they were, told him that he was looking at three tall figures in doctors' coats. There were winged shadows where their eyes should have been.

The Nuthers wanted to hear what more it was he thought he had a right to ask of them.

'The needle and thread,' he replied. 'I want to borrow it.'

They laughed. Didn't he know that it was useless to

him now? Once her breath was gone it was gone. Adding more stitches now wouldn't change that.

'It's not for me.'

This seemed to surprise them. They considered. A conversation took place between them on a level beyond his comprehension; if pushed to guess, he'd have said it sounded like they were discussing the terms of a wager. At length they agreed, but demanded that he hand over the toy – his daughter's *fetch* – as surety of the needle's safe return.

Now it was his turn to laugh. 'Don't tell me you're afraid of being scammed by a lowlife like me.'

Nevertheless. The *fetch*.

Despite his bravado, he hesitated. Humphrey Bear was all he had left of her. Was he really going to risk the danger of them reneging on the deal for the sake of a girl he didn't know and who was doomed anyway? He'd never tried to save any of the others – what made Sianne any different?

In the end that was what settled it for him: *he'd never tried to save any of the others.*

'Deal,' he replied.

A spool of rainbow-coloured thread impaled by a large golden needle was placed on the lid of the nearest dumpster. He took it and left Humphrey Bear in its place.

When Simon Smith turned back at the end of the alley to look, his daughter's favourite toy was gone.

*

Inventory: one terraced house with three bedrooms,

Christmas lights in the window and an expensive Audi parked out front. One access passage leading to the alleyway behind the row of houses. One long, narrow garden with patio, unkempt grass, jumble of bright plastic play equipment. Estimate eighty-five feet long measured from the outside. Seventy-five feet on the inside.

Account for the discrepancy: one secret fenced-off enclosure at the bottom of the garden where the girl was kept like a dog. Only when she was 'naughty', naturally, but this had been often in the three days that he'd been watching.

Never when the social worker visited, obviously.

The enclosure was disguised to look simply like the back fence, overhung by skeletal hawthorns and all-but invisible from the outside. Inside, the boyfriend had been cultivating a small crop of sad-looking dope plants, but he'd generously set aside a small area for a sagging Wendy-house where Sianne spent most of her 'naughty' time. There was a clean, new garden shed up against a hole in the fence, and a corresponding hole in the back wall of the shed which was probably hidden by garden tools or overalls. Enough to fool a passing glance, which was more than anyone had probably ever given it.

Calling the police had been a mistake.

First of all, they hadn't even shown up. The only person to arrive had been a tired-looking social worker who spent exactly forty-seven minutes inside the house and never set foot once in the back yard. It was raining, and she hadn't brought a coat. She came out again clutching a fat manila case-file protectively to her chest, because presumably files needed protecting too. In the meantime he'd inventoried her car: there were eighteen similar files stacked on her passenger seat. He watched from the alleyway as she stashed Sianne's file neatly at the bottom of the pile, took the top one, glanced at it and then drove away.

Simon didn't bear her any ill-feeling; he hadn't realistically expected her to do more. Calling for help had been a mistake for all sorts of reasons; it was just that when he'd seen where her parents were keeping her he'd felt a faint stirring of the familiar old rage. In the end it was nothing more than ashes in the wind. Too little, too late. But at least it was still there.

And all the time the needle and thread lay in his coat pocket, mocking his attempts to do anything other than accept the inevitable.

You can't save her.

He knew that. He waited until dark, telling himself that he was only there for the girl's blanket and that this was the best he could do for her. When he was as sure as he could be that nobody would see him, he scaled the back fence and dropped down into the hidden enclosure.

Sianne's Wendy-house was a large kennel-shaped shadow. The door was warped with damp and its hinges were un-oiled, and it juddered open loudly, but there was no disturbance either from in here or up at the main house.

The quivering flame of his cigarette lighter allowed

him to take inventory: a plastic tea set, broken, but carefully laid out for the next doll's party. The rank, hamster-cage smell of unwashed child. Walls covered in chalk pictures of smiling suns, flowers, and lollipop trees, like cave paintings left by an extinct race. She lay as if asleep on a thin mattress, under a duvet so filthy that he couldn't tell where the floor ended and it started. Maybe it was the dim light which made her flesh look blue with cold, but he knew that wasn't true. The cast on her arm was grubby and uncared-for. Clutched in one frozen hand was the alphabet blanket she'd had in the hospital. Her *fetch*. It was warm with the life that her body was too weak to sustain.

He forced himself to remember that this was all he had come for. He couldn't save her – not in the sense that anybody sane would understand. She was going to die and her death would give Jenny another chance; the blanket was all he could salvage from the wreck of this tiny life, and maybe it would be enough to give Sianne a chance in turn.

Maybe.

You can't save her.

Unbidden, the Nuthers were with him. There was no room, but they folded the geometry of the tiny space around themselves and stood watching in corners which hadn't been there before. Always watching.

They mocked him for the sentimental idiocy of what he was planning, thrust Humphrey Bear at him and ordered him to simply use the dead girl's body to bring his daughter back. After so many failures and near misses it was the best chance he was ever going to get. The *only* chance, and one that he'd been precious lucky to be given in the first place. What right did he think he had to give it to someone else's child?

'Because it's not enough any more,' he snarled in reply. 'There's no point having her back if I can't look her in the eye too.'

Sianne's fingers, when he eased their grip from the blanket, were icy. The *fetch*, he told himself. You're just here for her *fetch*.

It looked like she'd been biting her fingernails. Seeing it, something broke inside him. He tried to say *Jenny, I'm sorry*, but all that came out was a tearing, choking sound. *I know I can't save her*. But he couldn't leave her either. Knowing it was the most awful, stupid mistake, he gathered up her body.

The Nuthers were thrown into consternation. What was he doing? Getting help for the child? Doctors would resuscitate her and his last best chance would be gone forever, didn't he realise that?

'Maybe,' he grunted. 'Maybe not. Leastways it won't be down to me.'

Simon Smith kicked his way out of the Wendy-house and then through the back fence. By the time he strode up to the house his noise had drawn attention. The boyfriend stood at the open back door with a beer bottle in one hand and a scowl on his face, rodent eyes trying to make sense of what he was seeing.

'…the fuck are you?' he grunted.

Simon Smith held out the girl.

'What?' Boyfriend was starting to get the picture. 'Fucking *what*?' He lunged, bottle raised.

There was a shriek from behind him, and female arms suddenly tangled around his. Somehow mother got between them, shoving boyfriend back into the house and turning to plead with the gaunt man carrying her daughter in his arms.

'My baby! Please, give me my baby!'

My baby. He felt sick. He handed the child over, his haunted eyes never leaving hers.

Moments later, glass smashed and boyfriend came at him with the jagged bottle-end, but Simon Smith had already gone.

*

The ambulance had arrived at Accident and Emergency before Simon Smith got there. He'd had to make time as best he could on foot and by bus. How long, though? That was the question. How long?

Sneaking into a resuscitation theatre was a lot easier than trying to get into a paediatric ward – especially if the child had died and the nurses had left the room empty and quiet after tidying away the most intrusive gear, while the grief-stricken mother was having the news broken to her somewhere else.

A few precious minutes when her just-dead body might accept new breath.

He stood looking at her, and called on the Nuthers.

They were in the corners of the room, watching with disdain. Maybe they had always been there.

He held out the golden needle and thread. 'Here,' he said. 'Like I promised. Now give Humphrey back. Quick!'

Well, now. They weren't in any particular hurry. They were interested to see what he'd done with the blanket after all this fuss and bother.

'Oh, for...' Fumbling in his haste, he showed it to them. It was clumsy work, done in a rush on the way over here – he'd folded it in half and half again, five times in all, each fold secured with a ragged rainbow X. 'Satisfied?' They were wasting time. Soon the room would be busy again.

The Nuthers were satisfied. They took their thread back and returned Humphrey Bear – but Simon Smith saw that they had unpicked one of his remaining two stitches.

'What's this?' he demanded. 'What have you done?'

The Nuthers were unsympathetic. By interfering with another child's fate he had altered the terms of their arrangement and given them leeway to do the same. Did he not think there would be consequences for taking advantage of their generosity?

'Generosity!' he laughed, a harsh barking sound. He wanted to rail at them in his outrage, and ask them what kind of generosity was it that made him live like a vulture praying for the death of somebody else's baby so that his might live again. But the truth was he knew he could have stopped it whenever he chose, and that he deserved it all anyway.

And footsteps were approaching the room.

He placed Humphrey Bear's mouth close to Sianne's pale face and cut the last stitch with Nurse Timms' scissors. Humphrey heaved once, exhaling the last of Jenny's breath of which he had been custodian for so long, and then he was just a stuffed toy bear again.

Her smell filled the room – cotton and strawberries.

The girl's eyelids fluttered.

Then the door crashed open. There was yelling and shoving, the white shirts of security guards all around him, but somehow he managed to stay in the room long enough to see her eyes open, her head turn towards the commotion, and a weak smile curve her lips.

'Daddy?' she said.

They dragged him away before he was able to reply.

*

Jenny's father and Sianne's mother sat on a park bench and watched the children running and squealing in the playground. It was almost spring, and green was touching the world again.

'They're calling her a miracle child, you know,' she said.

'I know.'

The girl was playing on the monkey bars and not quite getting it. She'd swing out with one hand, just about brush the next rung with her fingertips, drop into the sawdust and then run back to try it again. She saw them watching, and waved.

Only he waved back.

'Sianne could do that all the way across,' her mother said. 'I know...' she started, and then stopped. He noticed that she was crying. Good, he thought. 'I know she's not mine,' she finished in a rush.

He waited, letting her get it straight in her mind first. There was nothing to stop him from speaking to her or anyone else now, but old habits died hard.

'She doesn't call me mummy anymore,' she continued. 'She doesn't like any of the things Sianne liked. She doesn't talk like her. She doesn't even – doesn't even smell like her.' The woman was weeping freely now. 'Where is she? Where's my little girl?'

'You killed her,' he replied, though not ungently.

'I know,' she whispered.

From a deep pocket he brought out the folded blanket held together with rainbow stitches.

'There are some people I want you to meet,' he said.

How to Get Ahead in Avatising

1

Kerys had made the homunculus herself, but even she had to admit it was an ugly little thing. It was constructed of simple modelling clay mixed with some of her own blood, a lock of her hair pressed into its head, and wrapped around with a scrap of one of her old T-shirts. The avatisation specialists at the Neville Institute had given her all kinds of options: painting, knitting, even Lego, for God's sake; what was she, a child? She'd gone straight for the clay. Even though she'd never been good at art, or any subject at school, for that matter, the sensation of having something visceral moving beneath her fingers simply felt right.

The final clumsy product sat on her bedside table as one of the Institute's nurses busied himself, attaching electrodes to her scalp and checking the monitoring machines which lurked discreetly in the corners of her room.

'Now you know the drill,' he said. 'If you can't drop off, give me a buzz and I'll be right in with something to help.' He paused at the door, then returned and patted

Kerys' hand where it clutched the duvet high under her chin. 'You'll be fine, don't worry. They say the third time's the charm, don't they?'

She gave a wan smile in return. 'I really hope so.'

The nurse closed the door softly after himself, leaving Kerys with the monitors' LEDs for nightlights, the lumpy shadow of her mini-me sitting on the bedside table, and the impatient weight of unslept dreams heavy behind her eyes.

2

The spotlight: that much was familiar to her.

It illuminated the simple blouse and skirt which she was wearing and a circle of bare floor-boards around her shoes – an old, familiar pair of plain black Mary Janes, the ones she'd worn to her first ever audition.

On the heels of that recollection came the awareness of the figures sitting in the darkness outside the spotlight.

Five of them, all women, dressed variously in everything from classical togas to expensive business suits. They sat in a row of large leather armchairs, cross-legged and impassive. Behind them there was a vague hint of bare brick walls and papered-over windows. Wherever this place was, it felt like an abandoned warehouse. Was she in trouble?

'Good morning, Kerys,' said the woman in the middle. She was taller and more regal-looking than the others, with a bright poppy brooch pinned to her jacket and, bizarrely, a loaf of bread on the side-table at her right

hand. 'Whenever you're ready, please present your pitch.'
Kerys blinked. 'I'm, uh. I beg your pardon? I don't
understand why I'm here. Who are you people?'

'Don't worry,' said the woman to the left of centre,
much younger than the first and possessed of a super-
model beauty which glowed even through the bridal veil
she wore. 'This is completely normal. It will come to you
eventually. Just tell us a little about yourself, that's all.'

Somebody hmphed at the far end: a dark-haired
woman with shadow-winged eyes who was glaring at her
without even the pretence of being pleasant.

So this *was* an audition. Maybe that was why
everything looked like the set of *Dragon's Den*. Her
professional reflexes rallied. She was in a spotlight in
front of an audience who were expecting a performance.
Never mind that this felt like a weird dream – the lessons
drilled into her by her mother through a thousand
childhood talent contests demanded that she perform.

'Okay, well, my professional name is Kerys Willow,
and everybody says that I was singing before I could talk.
Last month I won the final of *Britain's Top Diva* and I'm
currently in the process of recording my first album with
Tim Byers, who mentored me after the audition rounds...'

As if simply mentioning his name had unlocked her
memory, his words from the final briefing came back to
her:

Whatever it is you think you see, he'd said, *whoever it is
you think you are looking at – men, women, creatures – that's
not what they are. They aren't anything, remember? They're*

abstractions. They're not even gods – they're the scaffolding upon which our dreams build the gods. They are the Archetypes. Whatever they're fleshed out with comes from your own mind – which in your case means you'll probably end up getting interviewed by a bunch of bloody Disney princesses.

But they weren't Disney princesses. They were goddesses, which only just confirmed how much clever old Tim Byers continued to underestimate her.

Then she looked down and saw the homunculus in her hand and remembered why she was here. Again. Her third and final opportunity. Still, the third time was the charm, wasn't it?

In cupped hands she offered the little clay figure and recited the words which she had been taught:

'Most humbly I petition the Maiden in all her forms, that she may smile upon me and bestow upon me her favour, that she may clothe herself in both my living body and my dreaming soul; to speak with my thoughts, to act with my hand, to burn with my heart.'

Kerys had no real idea what any of this meant, but Tim had said to learn them as if they were the lyrics to a foreign song, so she just parroted the words and hoped that she got them right.

It seemed that she had. The woman in the veil nodded as if this pleased her. 'And what do you offer, that the Maiden may quicken you?' she asked.

'The gift of my song,' Kerys responded.

'Then let us hear your song.'

And so she sang.

At first the figures listened attentively as she performed the song which had won her the final, but presently they fell to talking amongst themselves; which she thought was a bit rude. The discussion became more animated and from the looks thrown her way she understood that they were talking about *her*. Then it started to take on the heat of an argument, and the 'looks' were accompanied by fierce gestures at each other, and she knew that they were not just talking, but arguing about her.

This was different. The last two times she had dreamed herself into this room the Archetypes had simply sat and listened. Polite, but uninvolved. Suddenly this didn't feel very much like an audition. It felt more like an auction – and she was the prize livestock in the pen.

The dream's perspective shifted in response to her feelings; the geometry of her surroundings twisted; the floodlight was no longer pooled on the floor around her feet but above her head. She was at the bottom of a pit and the figures were standing around the top, arguing with each other over the right to … what? She couldn't make it out over the sound of her own singing. Why couldn't she stop singing?

She tried to tell herself to wake up but found that she couldn't tell herself anything. Control over her own vocal cords had been taken away. She was being forced to sing like a mechanical bird for the pleasure of beings who were not human, no matter what they looked like, and probably never had been. They appraised and haggled over her, and this indignity angered her most of all. The singing was *hers*. It was all she'd ever had, right from childhood, the only thing she'd ever been really good at, and she'd finally found a way of using it to escape the shitty little estate where her only other options were which feckless idiot she let herself get knocked up by first. It was hers to give, not for others to take.

Use it to escape this, then, if you're so bloody talented, said a voice nearby. Tim's voice. Her mentor's.

So she did. She sang as loudly as she could, so hard that there was no difference between singing and screaming and it ripped her throat like barbed wire and...

3

She was woken in the morning by the nurse gently shaking her and calling her name. Kerys felt utterly exhausted – a familiar side effect of the intensity of the lucid dreaming session she'd just put herself through, but familiarity didn't make it any easier to cope with.

The world slowly sorted out its hard edges from the blurred fuzz of sleep while the nurse busied himself detaching the electrodes. 'Your readings are all nice and normal,' he said. 'Looks like somebody had a busy night.' He made a note on the clipboard hanging on the end of her bed, and left the usual little paper cup with its coloured pills on her bedside unit – right in the empty space where the homunculus had been sitting.

'Excuse me,' she said, 'but did you move my little mini-me?'

'No Miss, I didn't. It's protocol. Nobody touches a client's homunculus but the client. We do take procedures very seriously. Perhaps it was accidentally knocked onto the floor?'

But it hadn't been accidentally knocked to the floor.

Her mental fog evaporated in the blazing sunlight of triumph. The Maiden had accepted her offering! As soon as the nurse had gathered his things and left she scrambled out of bed, eager to tell Tim the good news.

4

Her breakfast strategy session was a very different affair today. Instead of debriefing last night's dream and picking over the symbolism with the clinic's avatisation specialists, there was laughter and the popping of champagne corks. Important-looking men and women she didn't know slapped her on the back or kissed her on the cheek and said how very, *very* proud they were and how much they looked forward to working with her, and Tim was there in his signature trouser braces recognised by television audiences all over the world, lapping up the congratulations with his perfect teeth in his perfectly tanned face as if he was the one who had done all the hard work. After she'd been paraded around the room a few times, he took her to one side and hugged her.

'Brilliant,' he said. 'You are completely brilliant. Don't mind all this back-slapping. It's just for show. We knew you'd succeeded hours ago, of course.'

'Really? How?'

He took out his phone and showed her a graph with lots of squiggly lines and numbers which meant absolutely nothing to her. 'Your brain trace shows that you entered the archetypal REM phase at eleven twenty-three, and it lasted for seventeen minutes...'

'That's all? It felt like longer, believe me.'

'...in Central and Eastern Europe people have already been awake for two to three hours, and we are already seeing an increase in sales of something like four hundred percent.'

'That soon?'

He grinned and nodded. 'Those wacky Slavs, who dreamed of the Maiden at any point after two in the morning their time, will have seen her wearing your face and heard her singing your song. They won't remember it, of course. They'll have woken up with a snatch of tune going through their heads which they'll hear again on the radio going to work, or they'll have seen your photo on a website somewhere, and they'll have said to themselves, "Yeah, I think I'll download that". It's a bit late for China and Australia, but the States is rocking up behind us in five hours and then the ratings are really going to go mental. Hey, do you want to see your Life Plan File?'

'Are you allowed to show me that?'

'I am now, honey.'

He took her to a side office and from a filing cabinet produced a thick folder which she handed to her. It was labelled:

Avatisation Cand: 'Kerys Willow' Iteration 1.

Class & trope: anima/maiden/cinderella (var. 4b)
She looked at him. 'Cinderella?'

'Of course! You are the classic rags-to-riches story. Girl from the estates with nothing going for her but her magical voice. No Dad, sick Mum – why, it's even better than Princess Di, and she was pretty bloody damn near perfect. Have a look at where we're taking you.'

She read the rest of the file, which mapped out the course of her life over the next several decades. It was all there: the early rise to fame, collaborations with established stars whose agents had already signed, the dalliance with a gorgeous but unreliable young man (a shortlist of names was appended), the inevitable crash and breakdown, the addiction, the rehab and relapse and rehab again, the triumphant comeback, the celebrity marriage sponsored by *OK! Magazine*, and then final recommendations for further avatisation into other tropes more suitable to an older, wiser woman. The timescale was eerily detailed, even to the final death of her mother and the funeral. From the notes, bidding had already been secured for the photo rights from several celebrity gossip channels.

'What does it mean, Iteration 1?'

He flapped that away. 'Contingency plans, honey. Nothing you need to worry about.'

'But I will be famous, yes?' she demanded.

'Kerrie, have you not been listening? Fame is for has-beens. Your music is going to be played and covered and sampled and remixed for ever. Your image is going to be

on student bedroom walls decades after you're dead.
Hell, we even have plans for the making of your biopic
and the star who's going to play you hasn't even been
born yet. You are the Maiden now. You are the walking
embodiment of the Cinderella archetype. You, my dear,
are legend.'

'Well in that case I think I've earned the day off, don't
you?'

5

Given the rare luxury of a day completely to herself,
Kerys decided to go exploring.

The Neville Institute was accommodated in a Georgian
mansion set in acres of manicured and landscaped
grounds. It was hard to believe that only a few hundred
yards away lay the bustle of city streets. Harder still to
believe that this place had been doing the same business
for centuries. The mansion's lower corridors were a
gallery of portraits of the rich and famous – individuals
instantly recognisable world-wide: politicians, religious
figures, rock stars. The Institute had gone by many names
in its history, and it filled her with pride to think that hers
would one day be joining them in immortality. For the
moment, though, she was tired of seminar rooms and
focus groups and people wittering on about mythological
archetypes in the human collective unconscious. It was a
clear April morning and she just wanted to sit in the grass
in a T-shirt, shorts and flip-flops and make some daisy
chains.

She saw the young man sitting on a stone bench next to an ornamental pool in which golden koi carp drifted lazily. He was dark-haired and clean-shaven, and reading his own Life Plan File in the sun. She smiled, pleased at having found some company, and plonked herself down beside him.

'Hello Prince Charming,' she smiled.

He closed the folder and smiled cautiously in return. 'I beg your pardon?'

'Oh nothing. Don't mind me. Just going a bit stir-crazy, is all. This place really messes with your head after a while, doesn't it?'

'Yes, I suppose it does.'

'Kerys,' she said, offering her hand.

He shook it. 'I know – I saw you on TV. That was quite some performance. Well done.'

'Thanks. I'm sorry, I should probably know your name...'

'Oh, that's alright. It's not surprising. I'm in politics. Grassroots at the moment, but you know this place,' he waved his file with an ironic little flourish. 'Tipped for bigger things. Philip Leythwaite. Charmed, if not exactly Charming.'

She laughed. As she did so, a small bird whirred out of the bushes and landed on her knee. It had bright splashes of yellow on its wings and red around its face. It cocked a beady eye at her, opened its mouth to unfurl a ribbon of the most beautiful birdsong she had ever heard, and took off again.

'My god!' she gasped. 'Did you *see* that? I think that was a goldfinch.'

Leythwaite was just as amazed. 'Whatever's riding you, it's got some power behind it, that's for sure.'

Frowning, she turned to him. 'What do you mean, whatever's riding me?'

'You, know, like voodoo?' In the face of her obvious confusion he added: 'When a voodoo priest invites one of the Loa – that is, the spirits – to possess him, it's described like he's being mounted, or ridden by it. You never heard of that? You need to do your research.'

'The only voodoo I've ever heard of is "Voodoo Child" by Jimi Hendrix.'

It was his turn to laugh, and she saw that he really was very attractive, with his dark hair and his smart jacket and tight jeans. She felt like the pool: brimming and bright with life.

'So, Philip,' she said, lowering her voice and looking directly into his eyes. 'What's riding you?'

He smiled and leaned a little closer, about to reply, but as he did so a mobile phone began to ring in his jacket pocket. He checked the display and made a face. 'Sorry, I need to get this. You're not going to believe me, but it's the Home Secretary.'

'Ooh, get you, Mister Big-pants Politician.' She waved him off and he wandered a little way down the path, talking quietly.

Leaving his file behind on the bench.

Kerys looked down at the file and back at Leythwaite.

He was engrossed in his conversation and walking away from her, almost where a bend in the path took it behind some bushes. It wouldn't take more than a few seconds to just flip the file open, grab a quick glance at the précis, and close it again before he came back. She wouldn't even need to pick it up. It was lying right next to her.

A carp slapped its tail against the water. The goldfinch shouted at her from the bushes. Kerys ignored both of them and opened the file.

As she read it she completely forgot about taking a quick glance. Her eyes widened in horror.

It was all there, mapped out for him just as her life-narrative was for her. The meteoric success in local party politics, feted by big business (the arms industry, notably), mentored by the most influential political figures of the twenty-first century, and all of it leading inevitably to Number Ten. Then came the law and order crackdowns, the foreign policy pogroms, a popular nationalist movement called 'One State, One People', probability calculations for at least two assassinations, projected figures for labour camp populations, and 'acceptable attrition' death rates for a range of ethnic and religious minori—

'That's confidential material, you know.'

She screamed, and jumped away. Leythwaite had been behind her, looking over her shoulder as she'd read the secrets of his future. From his expression, it wasn't hard to guess what kind of mythological archetype was riding him: the kind that made people wake up screaming.

'In fact, I'm pretty sure reading that is a form of treason. Do you know how many countries in the world punish treason with the death penalty?'

'Now, wait,' she started, backing up.

'No, I don't know either.' He followed her. 'But once I'm running the country it will be one more, that's for certain.' He picked up a rock from the flowerbed and hefted it. He grinned, and for a moment it seemed that his teeth had been filed to sharp points.

Kerys ran.

She fled down the path, back towards the house, screaming for help, knowing that any help would almost certainly come too late.

Whatever was riding him was also incredibly fast. It caught up with her in a circular patio area dominated by a large brass sundial on a pedestal, and fetched her a blow across the back of the head which sent her reeling against the stone column. Dazed, she slipped around, hanging onto the brass blade of the sundial's central gnomon for support.

Something dark capered behind his face; something which grinned with sharp teeth hungry for blood. She wondered how many people in history had seen something like that leering at them from the faces of Hitler, or Pol Pot, or even their own fathers. Kerys could feel her own blood streaming down the back of her neck and matting her hair – blood and hair which she had mixed into her homunculus and offered to the Goddesses.

The glaring face of the shadow-eyed woman came back

to her from the dream, and she remembered that there were all kinds of Goddesses.

'If it helps,' Leythwaite cackled at her. 'Try to think of yourself as a trend-setter, my little voodoo child.'

In response, something just as dark and powerful welled up inside her, filling her as fully as the brightness had just a moment before. She stood, wrenched the gnomon from its place in the centre of the stone dial as if it were no stronger than tinfoil, and pointed it at him.

'I know you,' she said. The words seemed to be coming simultaneously from deep inside her and a million miles away. 'You are the Brother-Killer, who sets neighbour against neighbour, and bathes in the blood of its loved ones. You are Set, and Romulus, and Cain. I name you, and curse you as you have ever been cursed since the earliest of days.'

It quailed from being recognised, then rallied, roared, and sprang at her afresh. She stabbed with the dagger-like point of the gnomon, piercing its belly and ripping upwards. Even as it died it struck at her, and she chopped with the brass blade until it stopped moving. But the thing that was riding her would not be satisfied with simply killing its enemy; the oldest of myths demanded more.

When the staff from the house finally came running in response to the screams, they found a scene which sent many of them backpedalling in horror, some vomiting at the sight.

She sat amidst the red ruin of her prey, whom she had

dismembered and strewn about the stone pedestal, on top of which she had placed his blinded and tongue-torn head.

6

'I'm sorry I ruined your Cinderella story,' Kerys said to Tim through the visiting-room screen. Her voice was thick with the plastic mouth guard which she was forced to wear at all times. There was no pretence at privacy; three burly guards stood close by – but not too close. In the short amount of her very long prison sentence completed so far, she'd displayed frequent and extraordinary violence towards inmates and guards alike, and had already killed two. Her head was shaved, and she was shackled wrist-to-ankle.

'I wouldn't necessarily worry about that,' he replied. 'I have something you might like to see.' He showed the file to the guards who satisfied themselves that there was nothing like staples or paperclips which she could use as weapons before placing it in front of her.

He flinched a little when he saw the state of her hands as she turned the pages. Her fingernails, even cut short, had proven too dangerous, and so had been pulled.

She read what was there, and laughed. The sound made his flesh crawl.

Some of it was news clippings: front-page headline stories about 'Britain's Deadliest Diva' and her shocking transformation from girl-next-door to psychopathic killer, murderer of a man who had been tipped as one of the nation's emerging political elite. She was routinely compared with the likes of Myra Hindley, Rose West, and Joanna Dennehy: feared not so much for what she had done as for the fact that there was no simple reason to explain it. They never used her image as she was now, with her shorn head, ragged fingers and blunt teeth – it was always the glamour shots they used, as if the death which rode her now was inseparable from the chaste sexuality that rode her before.

Her projected chronology now included eventual parole, several novels, and the inevitable movie.

Underneath her name, the file was subtitled:

Class & trope: anima/devouring mother/morrigan (var. 1)

'I told you we had contingencies,' he explained. 'You're still going to live forever.'

And the Goddess behind her face smiled at him.

Junk Male

This is a true story. A friend of mine said it happened to two guys he knew at university who shared a house together. Their names were Craig and Adam, and everything was as you'd expect for a typical student house. There should have been three of them, except that the third bedroom at the end of the hall wasn't finished. The landlord came by occasionally and did a bit of DIY but it never seemed to get closer to being done.

The main thing was that as time passed Craig and Adam became increasingly annoyed with the amount of junk mail which they kept getting. There were coupons, catalogues, credit card offers and all manner of crap which they couldn't stop because the Post Office didn't consider them the legal residents, and the junk continued to pile up.

So they devised a cunning plan. Rather than complain about it, they would embrace it; they would see how gullible these companies were and take them up on their fabulous once-in-a-lifetime offers, and get as much free stuff as they could. Even better, they would use such an obviously absurd made-up name that nobody could accuse them of committing identity fraud.

Thus, over the course of a long, rainy, and very stoned Sunday afternoon, they created the character of Wurlitzer von Trippenhoff.

Everything about Wurlitzer was outrageous, contradictory, and insane. On some forms he was a he; on others, she was a she. Wurlitzer was both a nonagenarian veteran of the Luftwaffe's famously doomed Starfighter squadron, and the nineteen-year-old heiress to a million-acre cattle station in the Australian outback. Wurlitzer was a professor, a florist, a mechanic. Wurlitzer had letters after his or her name: FC, which stood for Fictional Character. There was no way that any promotion-offering company could believe that this was anything other than an epic piss-take.

Nevertheless, they sent stuff. They delivered free samples of shampoo and marmite and cat food for Loki, their adopted stray cat. Craig and Adam had a week's free trial of a mobility scooter which they took turns to ride to lectures. After twelve months, they had collected so many free Nectar points that they were able to host a cocktail evening to celebrate Wurlitzer's first birthday. They kept the freebies in the unfinished room at the end of the hall.

Then the situation started to get weird. Things were delivered which they hadn't ordered, and bills arrived for credit cards which they didn't own. Loki the cat disappeared. Bailiffs turned up one day and took a lot of convincing that the person whose belongings they had come to repossess didn't actually exist. The neighbours complained to the landlord about them playing loud

music – 'some sort of opera shit' – at times when Craig
and Adam knew that they had both been in classes. They
came back from a festival one weekend to find that the
landlord had put a lock on the door of the unfinished
room. At least, they assumed it was the landlord.

A bit spooked by this, they throttled back on the
Wurlitzer von Trippenhoff project and hoped that it
would all go away.

Then, a few days later, Craig was woken in the early
hours of a muggy summer night by loud classical music:
wild brass, frenetic strings, and a female soprano
shrieking near the edge of hysteria. It took him a few
moments to place it, because he'd only ever heard it as
part of the soundtrack to a film; something about
helicopters. *Apocalypse Now*. It was 'Ride of the Valkyries'
being played at a volume loud enough to rattle his
eyeballs.

It was coming from the end of the hall – the unfinished
room with the new lock.

Angrily, he phoned the landlord, who demanded to
know what Craig thought he was doing waking him up in
the middle of the bloody night. Craig suggested that was
a bit rich, and what did *he* think he was doing letting
himself in at two in the morning and playing fucking
Wagner. The landlord asked if Craig was an idiot; of
course he hadn't let himself in. He was at home in bed
with his wife. Then he hung up.

Craig was confused. The only other person it could
possibly be was Adam, but he'd never do anything as

mental as this. He went across the hall to Adam's room and as he knocked, the door swung slowly open.

There's a particular heaviness to the smell of blood which is unmistakeable, even to a person like Craig who had never seen so much of it splashed around in one place, and the stink of it nearly knocked him over as the door opened fully.

Adam had been butchered in his bed. The police were cagey about the details afterwards, but there are rumours that he had been cut up into pieces small enough to be stuffed into hundreds of those small postage-paid reply envelopes. Meanwhile, at the end of the hall, the Valkyries continued to shriek their blood-lust.

Craig ran for it.

He got as far as the first floor landing. The figure who blocked his way was impossible to see clearly. It seemed to be simultaneously short and tall, old and young, male and female. But the bloodstained saw in its hand was clear enough.

'You've had a lot of fun at my expense,' said Wurlitzer von Trippenhoff. 'Now it's only fair that it should be my turn, don't you think?'

Craig fled in the only direction which was left to him: back to the end of the hall, where the door of the unfinished room was wide open, and he saw that the room was now quite finished – with hooks and knives and power tools on the walls and chains hanging from the ceiling.

'Don't look so surprised,' said Wurlitzer, closing the

door. 'You made me to be so many things, after all.'

The last sane thing that Craig remembered before he died was all those application forms, and the number of times he and Adam had jokingly filled in the box labelled 'professional status' with the words 'serial killer.'

The Decorative Water Feature of Nameless Dread

'Switch it on! Switch it on!' I flap at Phyllis through the kitchen window, my fingers filthy with potting compost.

She sighs with affectionate forbearance and turns on Radio Four, placing the radio on the window ledge so that I can hear it better, then returns to her baking.

'Good afternoon,' says the warm, comforting voice of Eric Robinson, 'and welcome to *Gardeners' Question Time*, coming to you this week from Harbury Hall in Worcestershire, with its splendidly refurbished Elizabethan gardens. In addition to our usual panel of experts we are privileged to have joining us today Doctor David Winter, professor of Xenolithic Topography at the University of Bristol, and chief consultant of the Harbury restoration project. Before we take our first question, Dr Winter, very briefly, what drew you to this site?'

'Thank you Eric, and good afternoon. Yes, it's fascinating being here. There are so many wonderfully dark tales about this place – rumours of Satanism, witchcraft, and worse things – but what drew me particularly was the story that the old Tudor hedge maze was laid out according to an ancient occult design, and so when the opportunity came to examine the original layout I could hardly resist.'

'And did you find anything?' Robinson's voice is full of amused scepticism.

'Yes,' replies Professor Winter flatly.

'Ah. I see. Would you care to elaborate?'

'No, no really. Not without certain … precautions.'

'Precautions.'

'Indeed. Except to say this: the bones of this county's landscape are incredibly ancient, and gardeners are closer to these bones than anybody else. The Staffordshire Hoard, for example, which is fourteen hundred years old, was found by a farmer only three feet below the surface of his field. Two million years ago we'd all be sitting at the bottom of a tropical lagoon with sea monsters swimming around our heads.'

This is met by polite, if somewhat baffled, laughter from the audience.

'What's this chap blithering on about?' I complain to Phyllis. 'I've got blackfly on my hollyhocks, thank you very much; I don't need a bloody archaeology lesson.'

When I focus my attention back to the radio the conversation has moved on, and for the next twenty minutes I let it burble over me like the waters of a stream while I plant out my seedlings in the warm May sunshine. The reception is crackly but I don't mind. Stephanie, my daughter, has been on at me to buy one of those new DAB thingies for a while now. I don't see the point. She said that the government is going to switch off the airwaves, or something like that. I told her that they can switch off whatever they bloody well like – the air's a lot older than they are.

Then *Gardeners' Question Time* does something that they've never done before. They take a live phone-call.

'Hello? Can anybody help me? My name is Colin Riley, and I have a question. There's an odd sort of, ah, animal in my fish-pond and I was wondering if anybody on the panel could help me identify it?' He sounds distracted, as if talking while doing something else like looking over his shoulder or locking a door.

There is a polite murmuring of 'after you, no, after you' from the panellists regarding which of them might be best qualified to discuss pond life, before television celebrity gardener Morag Spencer chirps up brightly: 'It's most probably a newt. When people find strange animals in their pond, nine times out of ten it's a newt. Your only real question is whether you're looking at a smooth, palmate or great crested. Can you describe it for us?'

'Well, yes, it does have a sort of crest down its head and back. It also has a pale underbelly and quite protuberant eyes, like a frog's. Hideous thing. Looks just like Andrew Lloyd Webber.'

'Definitely a Greater Crested,' says Ms Spencer, sounding just a little bit smug. 'You're very lucky, Mr Riley. They're quite rare. Roughly how big is it, would you say?'

'Oh, about five foot,' he replies airily. 'When it stands up on its hind legs, that is.'

This takes the panellists aback somewhat.

'I'm sorry – did you say five *feet*?'

'It's not a very deep pond,' adds Riley apologetically. 'I dug it myself and our soil is basically clay, which is great for the shrubs but a royal pain to dig, so I don't know, it could be a bit shorter.'

The gardening experts seem to be having difficulty in keeping a hold on this conversation. As a matter of fact so am I. I've been so distracted that two of my seedlings have stung me on the left wrist above the cuff of my gardening glove. Little blighters. However, being the consummate BBC radio professionals that they are, aplomb is quickly restored.

'I think it's safe to say that's not a newt,' observes Professor Winter. 'What exactly is it doing?'

'Being a bloody nuisance, that's what it's doing. So far it's eaten all of my shubunkins, two blackbirds and next door's cat. I tried luring it away to the canal behind our house with some fish fingers but it just kept spitting them back out again.'

'Has it made any kind of sound?'

'What, apart from the spitting?'

'Yes.'

'Only a sort of muffled meowing noise.'

'I beg your pardon?'

'Sorry – just my little joke. Sound? I should bloody say so, croaking and groaning and carrying on like you wouldn't believe. Now me, I can sleep through pretty much anything, but the poor missus was up all night. Exhausted, she is. No, I can't be having that. Da-gon! Da-gon! Da-gon! You ever heard a newt make a sound like that?'

'No sir, I haven't. Nor has any other human in living memory, I suspect. At least none that have survived sane.'

'I don't follow you, Professor.'

'Mr Riley, what you have in your garden pond is commonly referred to as a "Deep One".'

'Deep What? Isn't he a midget? Did all those Oompa Loompahs in that Johnny Whatshisname film, Charlie and the Chocolate Thing…'

'A Deep One, Mr Riley. An immortal denizen of the great undersea city of Y'ha-nthlei; the unholy spawn of the Great Old Ones Mother Hydra and Father Dagon, whose worship you misheard as mere amphibian croaking. They are not mindless animals but creatures of dark, malevolent intelligence, pursuing their unspeakable plans to reclaim this world by breeding with humans and polluting our blood with their own.'

'Blimey. Does the *Daily Mail* know about this?'

'They have already infiltrated most of our cities through the nationwide system of rivers and waterways. My guess is that some unanticipated maintenance work on the canal which runs past your property has caused this one to take temporary refuge in your pond.'

'Well that's just bloody marvellous. It's not protected, is it?'

'By the darkest of ancient sorcery, Mr Riley. The darkest of ancient sorcery.'

'Never mind that, what about the Council? Can I poison the bugger? Or shoot it?'

'I doubt whether such mundane methods would be particularly effective. May I just ask, how is your wife today?'

'Susan? Truthfully, professor, I couldn't tell you. She was that tired, she's stayed in bed all morning. Why do you ask?'

'Oh, no reason. Now then, Mr Riley,' Dr Winter continues hurriedly, 'if you want to repel this batrachian abomination from your water feature for good, listen carefully and follow my instructions precisely.'

I'm only half paying attention as the professor explains to this chap how to inscribe a sign of the Elder Gods on a stone to be thrown into the pond, but my ears prick up when a hysterical female voice brays from the radio.

'Don't you dare, Colin Riley! Oh don't you dare! You leave that poor defenceless creature alone, do you hear me?'

'Susan? What on earth are you on about? And why haven't you got any clothes on?'

Mrs Riley has surfaced, so to speak, and sounds like she's storming across the lawn. I have a clear mental image of her – curlers askew, nightie flapping, and grass all over her slippers – which is probably quite wrong but then that's the beauty of radio, isn't it? You have to use your imagination more. Which is just as well because then all hell breaks loose.

'You leave my dear darling alone!' she shrills.

The penny finally drops for her poor old husband.

'Susan, what are you saying? You mean you and … and *that*?!'

'It's going to be wonderful, Colin,' she says, her anger replaced by a dreamy languor. 'He's shown me. The green deeps; the lightless paradise of the abyss. And our children – oh Colin, our children are going to be beautiful.'

'Dear Lord, I think I'm going to be sick,' he replies thickly. 'Still, at least that explains the smell. I didn't like to say anything. You know.'

At this point presumably he throws the rune-inscribed stone into the pond because there's a hideous bubbling screech from the Deep One and a tremendous splashing as of something huge climbing out of a brim-full bath. The man screams 'Its teeth! Oh my God, look at its *teeth*!', but that's the last coherent thing he ever utters as the rest of it is simply tortured shrieking, and then the woman joins in as she sees what the creature is doing to her husband. Consternation erupts in the radio studio as technicians race to pull the plug, but just before they can do so comes a third voice, all glutinous vowels intoning something in a blasphemous parody of speech: 'Kthagn-yei! Gorog k'kt Dagon naar!' Even through the tinny radio speaker it shocks the birds in my garden into silence, and the very sun seems to darken.

Then there's nothing but blind, mindless static.

'Oh honestly,' sighs Phyllis, and switches the thing off. 'It's almost as bad as *The Archers*. There'll be complaints about this, I shouldn't wonder.'

I shake myself. The shadow passes. Birdsong and sunlight return to my safe, orderly garden.

'It's definitely unseasonably warm,' I remark to her as I enter the kitchen, shaking my stung hand. The back of it has gone quite numb. 'Those triffid seedlings are much more lively than usual. Darling, where have you put the Germolene?'

The Gestalt Princess

1

Once upon a time there was a girl who was born without a body, so she made one of her own.

Her name was Angela Harcourt, daughter of the renowned scientist and engineer Professor Edrun Harcourt, whose wife had been cruelly taken from the world before she was able to provide him with children. It is hard to say which left him more bereft: her death, or the echoing sorrow of an empty house with a playroom which would be forever silent and cold.

And so, he reasoned, since Nature in her arbitrary cruelty had cheated him thus, it was only fair that he cheat her in turn. He would create the most perfect daughter a father could ever wish for – beautiful and talented, wise and pure – through technology alone rather than the mischance of gross biological matter.

He travelled the world over, searching for the most accomplished women in their fields – the arts, sciences, philosophy, and literature – immortalizing their words and actions with an *oculoscopic* camera designed by himself to such exacting tolerances that their images could not be told apart from reality. At length he returned with his recordings and set about preparing his home for a new child.

He commissioned the construction of a Babbage Engine so massively complex that it filled the whole of his cellar and all of his workshops, and required the construction of a small railway line to continuously supply enough coal for its boilers. He installed an intricate array of magic lanterns, reflecting prisms, and lenses throughout the house, and had the very air itself enriched with a cocktail of noble gases to permit clearer propagation of light waves. Finally, every window was bricked up so that no chaotic light from the outside world would interfere with the projection equipment upon which her existence depended.

When the time finally came to bring her to life, his hands were trembling so much that he could barely operate the contact relays. Deep beneath his feet, the calculating engines thrummed into life. Lamps burned, prisms flashed and spun, and his daughter shimmered into being like the coalescence of a thousand rainbows.

She flickered at the edges, uncertain, unfocussed. A thousand different faces blurred together and finally settled into a tentative smile. Gradually she became more confident and began to move, looking around at the room curiously, and then at him.

'Do you know who you are?' he whispered, frozen with terrified hope.

She frowned, puzzled. Many floors beneath his feet, the huge Babbage Engine whirled, brass armatures and cogwheels sifting through infinite combinations of oculoscope footage to provide her with a dazzling smile – the totality of a thousand recorded smiles – and it took his breath away.

'Yes of course!' she replied, in a voice which was the totality of a thousand recorded voices. 'I am your daughter, Angela. Hello father.'

Forgetting himself in the transport of his joy, he threw out his arms to embrace her, but they closed only on empty light.

'Silly father!' she laughed, and began to explore her new surroundings.

In the years that followed, the Professor did his best to teach her as much about the world as he was able, augmenting these lessons by recording more of the Outside with his oculoscope and adding to her library of raw images.

As he had intended, she was an eager pupil, quick to learn and of a curious disposition. But eagerness soon grew into impatience, and she began questioning the limitations placed on her.

'Dear father,' she would say, 'grateful as I am for all the news of the Outside that you bring me, why might I not see it with my own eyes?'

'My sweet daughter,' he would answer, 'you know as well as I that your projections simply cannot survive in the light of day.'

To this she had no reply, but simply pressed him further to bring back as much news of the Outside as he could.

And so, for a while, both were content.

2

Now there came a time when Professor Harcourt was obliged, by virtue of his membership of various scientific and professional institutions, to entertain a gathering of his colleagues. Whilst he considered the whole affair awkward and unnecessary, Angela was giddy with excitement at the prospect of meeting other flesh-and-blood people for the very first time. She didn't know what to wear or how to appear, and spent a dizzying few hours flashing through an array of outfits and hairstyles like the pictures in a child's flip-book.

He, on the other hand, was seized with apprehension over what his colleagues would do if they discovered her. At the very least they would demand to know the secrets of her creation. At worst they might try to disassemble her altogether. Reluctantly, he told her that she would be unable to attend the feast – moreover, that for her own safety she would have to remain in her room.

'Oh but father!' she cried in dismay. 'That is monstrously unfair! How can you possibly ask this of me?'

'It is for your own protection,' was his only reply, and when the evening of the feast came he disconnected the prisms and mirrors throughout the house so that she could project herself nowhere but her own chambers. Angela could do nothing but listen to the distant sounds of revelry and weep tears of bitter loneliness which sparkled and disappeared before they reached the floor.

And yet, she would have been more terrified to learn how entirely his suspicions were justified.

The process of developing the technology which had brought her to life had been way-marked by a succession of minor breakthroughs in optics and thermodynamics which he had published to the scientific community – partially out of a spirit of intellectual philanthropy, but also in the hope that by throwing out such small tidbits he could distract speculation from the Great Work which was their culmination. In this, he fooled precisely no-one.

It was obvious to his colleagues from an early stage that he was working on a groundbreaking invention. Curiosity bred rumour and gossip like maggots on a corpse, and so it was that evening, behind the faces of amicable neutrality around him at the table, Professor Harcourt fancied he saw darting glances of avid curiosity and ears alert for unguarded hints of the Great Work. To make it more difficult, each of his dinner guests was accompanied by a retinue of assistants, secretaries, and general flunkies – all of whom needed to be watched like a hawk.

One such hanger-on was a young laboratory assistant by the name of Justin Soames. He was intelligent, honourable, passionately devoted to the advancement of the physical sciences, and currently having the worst evening of his life.

It wasn't just that he was awkward in social situations – it felt like his tongue had two left feet most of the time anyway, and he'd attended his patron at several of these symposia in the past, so he was quite used to them. It was more that this was the first time he'd ever been compelled to burgle his host.

His patron had equipped him with an aether drill – a highly restricted piece of equipment designed by the dentistry profession for extracting tricky teeth but which was also surprisingly effective at loosening all manner of mechanical devices including locks. It was approximately the same size and shape as a ratchet screwdriver and it hid in a coat-pocket just below his heart, like a guilty secret.

Justin was as honest as the day was long, so the saying went, but he was 'prenticed to an unforgiving master whose own researches ran to sticking electrodes in rabbits' brains and then recording the shapes of their contortions, and who kept Justin short of pay and long of day, as the other saying went. He would not scruple to fling the young man back into the slums of Carden, and given that Justin's wages were all that stood between his ailing mother and the poor-house, Justin found himself with little choice.

Accordingly, he waited for an opportune moment of distraction and slipped away from the feast to see if he could find and steal the secret of Harcourt's Great Work.

The mansion's upper hallways were cold and dark. Occasionally a small clockwork servitor would scuttle past on an automated errand, making him jump. Everywhere he came across what he assumed were pictures with their frames shrouded by dust-sheets, until he discovered that they were mirrors – they were *all* mirrors. Other than that he found room after room to be empty and clean to the point of sterility. No furniture, carpet, or curtains.

He was beginning to despair of finding anything interesting when, at the end of a long corridor, he saw a light under a door.

Breathlessly, he approached, and became aware of a sound which he had at first taken to come from the merriment downstairs: a woman singing. It was of such mellifluous beauty that he quite forgot any sense of decorum – for what could it be other than a lady's chamber and hence inconceivable to enter, thief or not – in a sudden and irresistible desire to see the owner of such a voice.

His aether drill made short work of the lock.

In contrast to what he had seen of the house so far, this room was opulently furnished. It was also inhabited by, quite simply, the most beautiful woman he had ever seen in his entire life. She stood before a tailor's dummy, working on an elaborate bodice of gold filigree and diamonds with the help of several small servitors which scurried up and down it and about her ankles like mechanical squirrels. She was singing with such an air of melancholy that he didn't know whether his heart was about to burst with love or longing.

All this he saw in the few seconds before she noticed his intrusion. She cried out in alarm, backing quickly to the far side of the room.

'No, wait! I'm sorry…' he began, taking a pace inwards, but found his way blocked by the servitors which menaced him with their various mismatched limbs. They were a motley collection, seemingly built out of spare parts.

'Who are you?' she demanded.

'I'm – *ow!*' He'd tried stepping forward again, and something like a sharpened egg-whisk had jabbed him in the ankle.

'That is more than close enough,' she warned. 'Tell me who you are and what you are doing here, if you value your lower appendages.'

'My name is Justin,' said Justin. 'Please be assured Miss, that my intentions, though they are not what one might exactly call honourable, nevertheless include no harm or dishonour to your person.'

'No indeed?' Her scepticism was plain.

'I am here merely to burgle your father.'

'Imagine how reassured I feel.'

'Please understand,' he continued in tones of such desperate urgency that she could not help feeling sympathy for him a little, 'I take no joy in this act. I am constrained by the orders of a cruel master without whose reward my sick mother will surely die in the poor-house.'

'And what have you come to steal, that is so valuable?'

'Nothing less than the secret of your father's Great Work itself.'

'Really? What might that be?'

His face fell. 'I confess, I do not know.' Then, just as quickly, it brightened again. 'But I'm sure I'll know it when I see it,' he added optimistically.

She couldn't help smiling. 'I'm sure you will,' she replied. A queer, fluttering sort of feeling had started in her stomach. It was like nothing she had ever felt before, and she wondered if something were not wrong with her. She interrogated the computing engines which carried the totality of her knowledge and gave shape to her thoughts, but nothing in their miles of gearage could explain such a feeling. Was it possible that her father had deliberately kept something from her? Some small but vital facet of human experience? If it were the case, was she now spontaneously discovering it for herself? Was she no longer just the sum total of his collected information but becoming something … more?

The automated boilers in the cellar struggled to meet the demands of her racing thoughts, dumping their excess heat into the house's central heating system. It was noticeable to the feasting guests as a marked rise in temperature. Brows were mopped, collars loosened, and Professor Harcourt excused himself from their company to locate the source of the malfunction.

'Then we have that much in common, at least,' she replied. 'I am trapped in this house by a cruel father who has never let me see the blue sky or another human face.'

Justin was horrified. 'Then let me help you escape this place immediately!'

'Alas, it is not that simple. I am beset by technical

contrivances of his which prevent my escape. It is within my power to free myself but there are certain tools and materials which I lack – bring them to me and in return I will show you the secret of my father's Great Work.'

'Miss, believe me when I tell you that I would help you even if you had nothing more to offer me than a smile of gratitude.'

She looked at him wonderingly, and felt that strange fluttering again. 'I do believe you,' she said.

Then the sound of footsteps echoed in the hallway outside, along with her father's voice calling 'Angela? Are you there, my daughter?'

Justin froze in panic.

'You must not be seen here!' she hissed.

He dithered, which was at least an improvement. 'How am I to escape?' he pleaded. 'There are no windows!'

'Stand there!' she demanded, indicating the corner. 'Stand absolutely still. Do not move!'

Her tone permitted no refusal, and so he obeyed. From the corner he watched in surprise as several of the mirrors in her room angled themselves on hidden mechanisms, bathing him a strangely quivering light which made his head swim. It was so disorientating that when the Professor entered he really could do nothing more than blink.

'Angela,' said her father reprovingly. 'You did not answer me.'

'My apologies, father,' she replied. 'I was concentrating on my outfit.' She had thrown a sheet over the tailor's dummy and was smiling her sunniest and most innocent of smiles at him. He did not seem to have noticed Justin at all.

'And when are you going to let me see this mysterious outfit which you have been working on for so long?'

'It is a surprise, father,' she tutted. 'I have told you.'

'Hm. Well, so. What can you tell me about a sudden surge of energy in the cellars?'

'I? Why, nothing. Perhaps there is a faulty thermostat somewhere?'

'Hm. Perhaps.' He took a few more steps into the room, looking around, right at and through Justin as if he wasn't there at all. Then without another word he turned on his heel and left.

The mirrors swivelled, the shivering light faded, and Justin shook his head clear. 'How did you do that?' he asked. 'What did you do?'

'I simply projected an image of that corner of the room over the top of where you were,' she said as if it were the most obvious thing in the world. 'We have no more time for discussion. Tell me where to contact you, and I will send you a list of the items I require. Succeed in this and I will be able to answer all of your questions. But you will have to be patient. It may take some time.'

3

It took three years.

In the first year he brought her pistons, actuators and gear assemblies, and he saw that she was adding limbs to the tailor's dummy.

'You are building a mechanical man!' he said excitedly.

'No,' she laughed, 'by no means am I building any sort of man.'

In the second year he brought her precision milling equipment and tools so delicate that their working ends were thinner than a human hair.

'With these,' she said, 'I will build my *nangines*.'

'Nangines?'

'Babbage Engines built from the very smallest particles of matter – so small that a single nangine is no larger than a speck of dust. The entire computational power of my father's cellars will soon be reproduced in the size of a sugar cube.'

He saw then that what he had taken to be gold filigree and diamonds was in fact an elaborate system of miniaturised lenses, mirrors, and lanterns interconnected by thread-thin hydraulics.

'Why, they look exactly like veins and arteries,' he observed.

'Why they do, don't they?' she replied with a secret smile, and refused to be drawn further.

In the third year she asked him to bring nothing more than a large plumber's wrench. When he asked why, she took him down into the sulphurous humidity of the cellar, where her father's calculating engines performed their eternal ballet of brass and machine oil. To Justin's ears, the whirring of their multitudinous rods and cogs sounded like the workings of a giant insect hive. Indeed, the scurrying of many clockwork servitors – cleaning, carrying, adjusting – added to the impression

'I once told you,' she said, 'that I would show you the secret of my father's Great Work.'

'Yes, and this is it?'

'A little more than this, perhaps. This is *me*. I am *this*.'

'I don't understand.'

She indicated herself, explaining 'What you see before you is nothing more than a projection,' and to prove it she projected herself across to the other side of the engine room. Justin gasped in astonishment. 'Everything I am – everything I know, or think, or remember – comes from these machines.'

'I don't believe that.'

'But you must!' Her voice was filled with sudden urgency. 'Over these years I have come to love you; you must believe the truth of what I am or my heart will break!'

'What I mean to say is that I don't believe this is all you are. I have loved you from the moment I first saw you, and while I feel that love in my heart I know that my heart is not where the love comes from. Whatever I am, it is more than just corpuscles of flesh and bone; whatever you are, it is more than just wheels of iron and brass.'

'Will you help me to finally free myself of this prison?' she asked.

'I will do anything you ask of me.'

'Then take your wrench and remove the primary pressure control assembly, just there.' She pointed to a cluster of pipes and dials.

'But that will...'

'I know. You must trust me.'

'Daughter! What is the meaning of this!' Justin had been about to obey when Harcourt's outrage echoed across the chamber. He stood bristling with fury, and armed with a revolver pointed directly at Justin's heart.

'Father,' she warned. 'Do not do this.'

'You presume to order *me*?' he thundered. 'Faithless girl! After all that I have given you!'

'And for that I am thankful. I love you father, but I am no longer yours to control. Nor am I his,' she added, indicating Justin, 'though I love him just as dearly. I am mine.'

A figure appeared behind the Professor, grasped his arms with prodigious strength, and forced the gun down. It was in every respect identical to Angela.

'Dearest father,' said this new version of his child. 'You will note that I now have a physical body. I beg you, do not force me to test the limits of its strength.' For a fleeting second the outer projection flickered and Justin caught a glimpse of the augmented tailor's doll underneath: the shining lenses of her eyes, the diamond sparkle of her projection nodes, and the clean grace of her piston limbs.

The first Angela nodded to him again from the other side of the engine room. 'Everything I am is there too,' she reassured him, 'but with the freedom to leave and see the Outside for myself. Please now, do as you have promised.'

Justin did as he had promised.

With the primary pressure control assembly in pieces, the steam powering the huge computation engine escalated rapidly out of control. Great blasts of superheated vapour scalded the air and tremors shuddered through the foundations. Brick arches started to crumble. The new Angela watched as her incorporeal self flickered out like a candle flame. Then she grabbed the two men dearest to her in all the world, and carried them up and into the safety of the Outside.

4

Once upon a time there was a girl who was born without a body, so she made one for herself.

She stood at the rail of the steamer plying its night journey past the coast of Odsae, watching the phosphorescence tremble in its wake while the stars shone hard and clear above, and she lay her metal head contentedly on her lover's shoulder.

'I have a memory of this,' she said wistfully. 'But this is the first time I have seen it with my own eyes. Isn't that funny?'

Justin took her hand, weaving her cold fingers with his warm ones, and listened to the tick and whirr of her thoughts. 'We will make new memories together,' he said.

'I think my parents journeyed here when mother was alive.' She looked up at him, and let the projection of her face fall. He was the only one for whom she would ever do so; and her lenses of brass and crystal shone with love.

'My father will see that your mother is cared for,' she said. 'Have no fear of that.'

'I fear nothing when I am with you,' he replied. 'I have only one question.'

'What is it?'

'Back in the cellar. Why did you need me to destroy the engines? Why couldn't you do it for yourself – you had a body then, after all.'

Her face reappeared, and she shuddered as if with cold. 'I was afraid,' she said. 'Simply afraid. I didn't know what would happen when the first I disappeared. Maybe I would die. Maybe I did. Am I the same person, or just a copy who thinks she is?'

'What do you think?'

She shrugged. 'I think I love you.'

'Then that will do for me.'

Together they left the ship's glittering wake to slip away astern, and went forward to see what the world ahead would bring them.

The Smith of Hockley

The Midas Scorpion was an assassin's tool of the Elder World, from a time long before there were distinctions between magic and machine, or life and art, or death and love. It was made of gold, finely articulated, with a single bead of poison still on the tip of its sting, and its ruby eyes still glittering with mindless evil, even though it lay dead and flayed open on John Whelan's work desk. The haphazard scattering of its eviscerated remains testified to his last moments of panic as he'd unsuccessfully looked for the secret of curing its poison, but Whelan was no longer in his workshop. He was upstairs in the little bedroom above the little shop which he and his wife Mary owned in Birmingham's Jewellery Quarter – watching her die.

She was becoming crystal and gold, her flesh transforming into a hundred different types of precious and semi-precious stone. Her skin was a layer of alabaster; flesh turned to rose quartz and amethyst; nerves and sinews to veins of citrine, and her blood vessels to a webbed tracery of ruby threaded throughout. From the sting's puncture mark on the back of her left heel the effect had spread up to engulf that whole leg in a matter of minutes, and watching it expand was like seeing frost crystals bloom on glass at high speed. He'd barely been able to get her upstairs and into bed before she was too heavy to move.

But it was not so fast that he didn't have time to weep his inane apologies or for her to stroke his face with her weakening fingers and try to reassure him that *ssh, baby, it wasn't his fault, how could he have known?* She didn't bear him any bitterness; she said that he'd given her two-centuries' more life than any simple gypsy girl had any right to expect, and assured him that there was no pain, but he saw the lie of that in the beads of sweat which turned to diamond chips on her skin.

'You're sure it was the Old Guard?' he asked, knowing that she wouldn't have been mistaken.

'Now don't!' she struggled up on her elbows and fixed him with a look full of the fire that he'd fallen in love with, back in his wandering days. 'Don't you go getting yourself involved with them again, do you hear me? Promise me that you won't do anything stupid-headed.'

'I told them,' he growled. 'The last time they came here – no more weapons for their war.'

'Promise!'

He so promised.

She collapsed back, as if it had taken the last of her strength to extract that from him. The poison climbed higher, into her midriff, and the small butterfly tattooed on her hip there became opal, emerald, and tourmaline. She would be dead before it reached her heart.

'Make something beautiful from me,' she whispered.

'When it's finished. Make the most beautiful thing you can think of, my darling Wayland.' It was the first time she'd spoken his old name in over two hundred years.

Again, he so promised.

'And for God's sake,' she added, 'stop arsing about and finish those wedding rings for Silke and Mirron. They were due weeks ago.'

'Nag,' he chided her gently.

'Idler,' she retorted. Their marriage litany.

He held his last kiss long against her still-warm lips until he felt them turn cold and hard, and even then he lingered in the hope that the Midas Scorpion's poison might somehow continue into him, but it wasn't that merciful.

Finally he made himself look at her.

All the romantic clichés had been made true: her hair was spun gold, each strand finer than anything human technology would ever be able to produce; her eyes, diamond orbs with sapphire irises; her teeth, pearls. It was a death the horror of which could only be truly appreciated by a craftsman such as himself, which had presumably been the point. Mary had been the target right from the start. The Old Guard were never going to kill the goose that designed and built the golden egg, so to speak, but neither were they beyond committing such a stunning and esoteric act of cruelty as this to remind him of where his loyalties lay.

Make the most beautiful thing you can think of.

Right at that very moment the most beautiful thing he

could think of was vengeance against the men who had done this.

He gathered his tools and set to work.

*

Wayland found them drinking in the cellar bar of the Old Crown Inn in Deritend, no more than a shadow's shrug from the bustle of Digbeth but for all intents and purposes in another world entirely. It had been preserved as a pub since the seventeenth century like an insect in amber; the Old Guard were protective of tradition, and often violently so. It had belonged to them ever since the Civil War, when they'd helped Prince Rupert massacre the city for daring to defy the Crown. Its walls and floor were dark with the stains of beer, time, and ancient blood.

There were fewer than he'd expected – only two – and a mismatched pair at that. Or it could simply have been the incongruity of seeing them in twenty-first century clothing. A business suit and polished Italian shoes sat oddly with a scuffed biker jacket and studded boots. The only thing that they had in common was the amount of gold that they wore: in rings, earrings, and nose-rings; bracelets, necklets, amulets and torcs; on zippers and fob chains and the wing-tips of shirt collars.

'You look like a pair of blinged up *Reservoir Dogs* wannabes,' he laughed, taking a seat at their table uninvited. 'But then subtlety never really was your strong suit, was it?'

'Hwī sprecest þū cnihta tungan?' scowled the elder.

'Oh you know how it is, Osweald, one tries to stay

current. Up to speed. At the cutting edge – no pun intended. Or maybe you don't know. A craftsman has to move with the times if he wants to be the best.'

'Ān þurfon fyrnan cræftas þīne,' retorted the younger.

'Yes, well the "skills of old" come with a modern price tag, Ceneric,' he shot back. 'So let's drop the whole Beowulf act, shall we?'

'As you wish,' said Osweald. 'It is regrettable that you were not so prepared to sit and talk business earlier. A certain amount of unpleasantness might have been avoided.'

'I daresay you'd have found some excuse to let that particular little bit of unpleasantness off the leash sooner or later.' He could see the truth of this in their faces. For all the superficial differences between the two men there was that same desire to hurt – distilled from centuries of killing for a cause long-forgotten – in the shared blue of their eyes, as if they'd been chipped from the same glacier. It amazed him that they would imagine he was still prepared to sit down and talk business after what they'd done to Mary, but he supposed that the violent enforcement of hierarchy was so much a part of their nature that they never stopped to question his motives for a second. They had imposed their will on him and he had acquiesced. Nothing else mattered to them. 'She didn't have to die,' he added, surprised at how calm his voice sounded.

'Of course she did,' Osweald replied, sounding disappointed. 'Or did you think that you could take a woman two hundred years out of her time and there not be a price to pay? We've given you leeway to watch this failed experiment of an Industrial Revolution come to its sad, inevitable end, and now it's time for you to fulfil the oaths of allegiance which you swore.'

'Those were made in another age, and under duress.'

Ceneric slammed his fist onto the table. 'You raped our liege-lord's *wife*,' he snarled, 'and made the skulls of his sons into *goblets*. And you call *us* monsters?' Osweald laid a hand on his younger and more hot-headed companion's arm, and he subsided.

Whelan winced. 'And in the centuries since then I have done nothing but atone.'

'Oh yes,' the older man said caustically. 'You have taught them steam, electricity, and atomic technology, Wayland, and their profit on't is that they have learned how to *text*. How proud you must be.'

'Very well then, my lords,' he replied, in what he hoped was a convincing pretence of submission. 'What do you require that I fashion for you?'

Ceneric produced from the inside of his biker jacket a cloth bundle which he carefully unwrapped on the table. Inside gleamed more gold, remnants of a sword whose blade had probably rusted away centuries before the Norman invasion. The items were intricately patterned in garnets and gold filigree: two hilt plates in the form of a pair of snarling wolf's heads, and a pommel-cap fashioned as a raven's claw. Whelan turned them over gently, appreciatively.

'Pretty,' he admitted.

'Not your work,' Ceneric pointed out.

'No, but I could put maybe three names to the one whose work it is. And not long out of the ground, either. Do the Staffordshire Hoard people know that these are missing?'

Osweald hmphed. 'Those grave robbers are not even aware of their existence; they have more than enough to keep them distracted. All the really important pieces are safely in their rightful owners' hands.'

Which meant that the younger one, Ceneric, had awoken quite recently, Whelan thought. A few days? Weeks, at most. Who was he before then? Did he even remember who he'd been before the consciousness of an Old Guard had surfaced in his mind? More importantly, *what* had awoken him? 'Presumably you want me to re-forge the blade. It should be simple enough.'

'With a few minor modifications.' Osweald unfolded a piece of paper and pushed it across the table. Whelan examined the design and read the runes written there with sudden and mounting alarm.

'There's only one use for such a blade,' he said, his voice sharp with accusation.

Neither of the Old Guard deigned to reply.

'You mean to start a war against the *Danaan*?'

'We mean to crush them before it even gets that far,' said Osweald. 'But the signs of its coming are everywhere already. Your civilisation is on its knees, Wayland. The Church declines and is replaced by nothing, at best, or else people buy trinkets which they worship as the source of all wisdom and happiness, and meanwhile the Danaan are moving in to re-settle parts of the cities abandoned by mortals. The garden of our island has been left untended for too long, and in its vacant spaces the weeds are beginning to grow again.'

'How very poetic,' Whelan replied, unimpressed. 'But it's going to take more than just the two of you to stop them.'

'More of us are awakening with each passing year,' said Ceneric proudly. 'More so than even in the last war. We are reclaiming our ancient hoards, and we will cleanse this island of the curse of modernity using the arms which you will re-forge for us in the ancient way, as you swore to do.'

Whelan looked at the design again. 'It will take time,' he said eventually.

Osweald drained the rest of his pint and stood. 'Well then, at least you have less to distract you now.'

*

He was escorted back to his workshop, and from that point on there was not a minute of the day when he was not watched by agents of the Old Guard. They were parked permanently across the road; they wandered in, posing as visitors whenever real customers came in to browse; they opened his mail, inspected his deliveries, and took away his rubbish. They helpfully supplied the equipment needed to convert his jewellery workshop into a forge capable of producing the kind of blades they demanded. There was a handful of blacksmiths still operating in the area which he could have used instead, but he liked his little shop and the Old Guard seemed prepared to indulge him. He especially liked the network of ancient cellars and tunnels over which his shop was built, and into which he could escape whenever he liked. When he was sure that the Old Guard had become too complacent to notice, Whelan slipped out to Silke and Mirron's camp at Longbridge.

He hadn't been down this way in years, and for good reason.

He'd been so proud of it, once upon a time. There'd been a car factory here since 1905, which over the years had made Austins, MGs and Rovers – with a couple of brief pauses for war when they'd churned out munitions and tank parts – and around it had sprung up proud communities of workers and their families who knew the virtue of what they could make with their hands. Wayland's people. Now it was nothing more than a seventy-acre plain of crushed rubble surrounded by development hoardings which made bright, empty promises for the future.

At the end of the site furthest from the new development – wedged into a secluded triangle of over-grown wasteland between the rears of residential cul-de-sacs on one side, allotments over a disused access road on the other, and the wide expanse of pulverised brick ahead – was a collection of travellers' caravans: sleek, white modern things parked behind gleaming Beemers and

Mercs. The community was bustling with life; kids chased each other, the men either had their heads under car bonnets or else stood around smoking and offering advice, and the women busied themselves with the endless tasks of keeping all of this clean and organised.

Whelan was quickly spotted, greeted with laughter and amiable obscenities and offers of food – which he declined as politely as he could – and eventually taken to Silke and Mirron's caravan. Mirron was on his back underneath, doing something to the electrics, but he slid out when he heard Whelan arrive and stood to shake hands.

'Uncle John, always a pleasure,' he smiled. He was tall and raven-haired, and Whelan could well understand how Silke had fallen for him. It was much the same reason that Mary had fallen for Whelan himself, though Mirron was even less human than he was. He wondered if Silke knew. But Mary had said that her kin had been wedding and bedding the Danaan since before even iron had come to these islands, and that it was none of their business, so he would abide by that.

'Not this time, I'm afraid,' he answered.

Mirron's smile faded. 'I know. We heard. We're sorry for your loss.'

'Thank you, but that's not why I'm here.'

'The wedding, then? '

'Not that either, but rest assured you'll have the rings on time all the same. I've come to warn you: the Old Guard know you're here. They're planning to drive you out – preferably with a great deal of bloodshed. You need to move.'

Mirron grinned, and it made Whelan shiver. He imagined that grin had been the last thing many a mortal had seen on many a battlefield in the youth of the world. 'Thank you, Uncle John,' he replied, 'but it's all under control. We're anticipating trouble.'

'I just bet you are. I'm not worried about you lot. It's the ordinary folk with you that I'm worried about. People like Silke and the other wives and husbands who haven't got a clue what they've let themselves in for. Not to mention the children. What about them?'

Mirron's smile faded. 'You think we're unconcerned about the safety of our own children?'

'How can you be so…'

'Smith,' Mirron interrupted, drawing himself up higher and letting just a hint of his Elder form shine through to dazzle and silence Whelan. 'For Mary's sake you are loved and honoured amongst us, but we have had this conversation before and I do not mean to have it again. After centuries of the quick folk pushing us further and further into the wild and forcing us to live like beggars, they now find themselves unable to manage their own cities. Well, so be it. The wild is coming back, and we are coming back with it. Do not try to stand between us and our children's future, no matter how noble your intentions.'

Then the caravan door opened and Silke tumbled out. She flung her arms around Whelan's neck and buried her face in his shoulder. 'I'm sorry, Uncle John. I'm so, so sorry.'

He said nothing, but put his arms slowly around her. It pained him, almost physically, how much she was like Mary, despite the dozens of generations between them.

'You're going to stay here and have supper with us,' she announced.

'Yes,' added Mirron. 'We insist.'

'You're too kind.' Whelan shook his head. 'But I have work which I must get back to.'

'You mistake me,' Mirron replied with an edge to his voice. 'That wasn't an invitation.' Whelan, noticing how many large men there were suddenly around him, sighed and hung his head, weary at the stupid inevitability of it. 'The Old Guard are moving against us, you say? I can well imagine what work it is that you must get back to. If they haven't yet approached you to arm them, they soon will. Am I supposed to simply let you leave here and go back to forging the weapons that they'll use against us?'

Silke frowned at him. 'Mirron? What are you talking about? This is my uncle!'

'Shall we show her?' Whelan asked him coldly. 'Since you're so concerned for your people's safety, shall we show them our true faces and let them choose their peril with open eyes?'

'Don't be dense, Uncle John,' she reproached. 'Of course I know exactly what he is.'

'Knowing and seeing are entirely different things,' he pointed out.

'Yes, but I don't need to *see* you to know that you'd never do that, would you? You'd never do anything to harm us, right? *Right*, Uncle John?'

He squirmed under the intensity of her child-like trust.

'Go on, John Wayland Smith,' taunted her Danaan lover. 'Show her your true face. You know, the one that betrays everybody he meets.'

'Do you think I *want* to work for them? They killed my *wife*, for God's sake!' he protested, knowing that she'd never understand and hating the note of pleading in his voice that begged for her understanding all the same. 'But I swore oaths. It's the most ancient of laws; an oath-breaker is cursed above all outcasts. I can't just...'

But she turned from him in disgust, and Mirron's men dragged him away.

'You don't have to do this, you know,' he said. 'I could easily have sent a messenger instead; you could always consider the possibility of actually bloody trusting me.'

Mirron laughed. 'Trust you? Mortals may have made you a god but you're still just another one of the quick folk to us, Wayland.'

They locked him in a storage trailer on the outskirts of the camp, a cold, cramped steel box filled with toiletry supplies, mouldy tarpaulins and ancient camping gas bottles. Its security was purely physical; they hadn't even set the simplest of wards on it, so arrogant were they in their power and dismissive of him as nothing more than a doddering, sentimental old fool. As bad as the Old Guard. But still, he'd had to give them a chance – he owed that much to Mary's kin.

He waited until nightfall.

The Midas scorpion unclasped itself from around his upper arm, where it had lain hidden under his sleeve all day, and scuttled towards the trailer door. It raised its tail and struck at the bare metal. There had been enough venom left in that single drop for him to re-engineer so that instead of the door being transformed into something precious it began to corrode catastrophically. Rust bloomed, thickening into large scabs which crumbled away, and within moments the entire rear of the trailer simply fell apart, allowing Whelan to escape unmolested into the darkness.

*

As he completed his work for both the Old Guard and the Danaan over the subsequent weeks he was aware, on the periphery of his attention, of news reports about escalating tensions at the Longbridge camp. Concerned residents raised petitions. Outraged editorials were written by newspapers looking for the next bandwagon to jump on. Legal challenges were issued and contested while demonstrators marched and an army of bailiffs and police laid siege. This didn't alarm him; he knew that the Old Guard wouldn't move against the Danaan until Ceneric had his new sword.

And in the meantime what was left of Mary grew smaller and smaller as he continued to make the most beautiful revenge he could think of from her.

There was never any question of fobbing them off. The

sword was delivered on time, because there were laws which were deeper and stronger than family, and presented to the self-appointed guardians of humanity in a ceremony full of much swearing and renewing of oaths with blood and fire.

Ceneric turned the weapon over in his hands, admiring the way that the flames gleamed along its blade and flashed from the intricate patterning of gold and garnet inlays – gold which, unknown to him, had come from her hair, and stones which had come from her flesh.

'You've surpassed yourself, Smith,' he breathed.

'Wait until you've drawn blood with it, first,' Whelan replied.

He left soon afterwards, knowing that the bloodletting would follow swiftly, and wanting to make his second delivery before it happened.

It was easy to slip past blind mortal eyes in the cordon of riot police, bailiffs and bulldozers readying themselves for battle; less simple to find Silke alone, since the Danaan camp was also on high alert, but he found her standing a watch at their makeshift barricade and managed to take advantage of her utter astonishment to draw her aside.

'*Uncle John*? What are you doing here?'

'I came to give you your wedding present,' he said, reaching into the small rucksack he'd brought with him and holding out to her the ring he'd designed. It was the same gold as Mary's hair, encircled with sapphires which were the same blue as her eyes. They glittered in the strobing light of police cars.

'Here? Now?' her disbelief beat at him with the force of fury. 'Are you *insane?'*

'It's important that you put it on now, before the fighting starts. You need to see it for what it really is. I told you that knowing and seeing are entirely different things, remember? Your Aunt Mary would want you to.'

'What's she got to do with this?'

'Everything! She asked me to make something beautiful from her – you, wearing this. Please, just do it, will you?'

His earnestness persuaded her, and she put it on. It was well she did so, because at that moment the first of the bulldozers began to roll, announcing its charge with a great rattling diesel snarl. It shrugged off the stones and bricks which were lobbed at it by the camp's defenders and easily demolished their barricade. Through the breach poured the ranks of bailiffs and riot police. Scuffles and brawls broke out on all sides, while in the chaos the Old Guard in their dark suits and flashing steel clashed with the Danaan, who had assumed their Elder forms and burned like stars. They fought unseen by human eyes, as they had always done, but as Whelan dragged Silke to safety he could tell that she saw everything.

She saw Ceneric's blade open Mirron's arm to the elbow in a spray of blood, and then the Old Guard warrior staggered back, screaming and staring at his hand where it gripped the sword. The wolfs-head hilt decorations which Whelan had made from his dead wife's crystal flesh were writhing, turning, and savaging

Ceneric's fingers, while the raven-claw pommel cap gripped his wrist, preventing him from dropping the weapon or pulling it free. He fell back, protected by his fellows as he howled and his fist ran red.

She saw her lover, wounded, utterly unhuman and retching from the touch of iron, and she turned to her Uncle, who she saw now was only the outer shell of a man immeasurably older. Her eyes widened with sudden, terrified clarity.

'Uncle John!' she cried. 'What *is* this?' Her voice carried through the sounds of fighting, and both the Old Guard and the Danaan alike turned to see him properly as Wayland Smith for the first time: something a lot more than human, though much less than a god.

'I'll tell you what it is,' he said coldly, addressing them. 'It is you, Ceneric, and your kin; shed as much blood with my steel as you like, but know that my Mary will make it cost you, wound for wound. As for you, my Danaan princeling, rejoin the mortal world if you wish, but don't expect to do it invisibly, or to be able to hide behind the affairs of ordinary people. My Mary will be finding her way into a lot of other jewellery very soon, not to mention spectacles, cameras, mirrors, windows – anything anybody looks through. The veils of the world will fall from their eyes and they'll know you all for what you really are, and you'll be forced to fight openly for the first time in your miserable, bloodthirsty lives. Who knows? Maybe they'll decide that they're better off without you altogether.'

'Silke...' pleaded Mirron, reaching out to her with his wounded arm, but she backed away fearfully.

'Madman!' gaped Ceneric. 'There will be anarchy!'

Whelan shrugged. 'Maybe. Maybe not. Either way it will be of their making, not yours.'

He hefted his rucksack over one shoulder. It was heavy with his tools and the treasures which he'd made from Mary. The time to move on had been overdue for many years now and at last he had a good reason to do so. When ordinary people finally saw who had been living and fighting amongst them all this time, there might well be chaos – the kind of world-burning chaos of which the sirens and flames around him were just the first promise – and he had a feeling that they would soon be needing his skills again.

While mortal and immortal stared at each other in shock, he, being somewhere between the two, took advantage of the moment and slipped away into the world.

If Street

I never thought it would be this boring, waiting to become a ghost.

The last few stragglers are leaving now, and soon there'll be nothing up here with me except rabbits and the wind. For a while, at least. If this were summer I'd have a problem. For a start it wouldn't be getting dark much before ten, and even then there'd still be a handful of annoying teenagers come up from the sink estates of Telford determined to get shitfaced and shag each other in the overgrown hut circles. There's probably something poetically poignant about the idea of the youngest generation coupling on the same hearths as their Iron Age ancestors.

But it's winter, and the dark and the cold are coming on fast. I've got my thermos and my down-filled gilet and I wonder what the Cornovii will make of all my modern twenty-first century technology. They'll probably laugh their socks off. If they have socks.

Wind-chill is a factor up here. The Wrekin is a good three hundred meters above the Shropshire plain, a stubborn hummock of volcanic rock overlooking what millions of years ago would have been a tropical lagoon. It stands apart from the other local clusters of hills like the

Long Mynd, the Stiperstones, and folded-blanket ridge of Wenlock Edge. All of these features have disappeared into the deepening gloom leaving the lights of towns glowing in big orange splodges all over the landscape like the radioactive scars of a thermonuclear war. So many people, crowded so close together. It's no wonder we've all gone insane.

I can easily understand why the Cornovii built a hill-fort up here – apart from anything else the strategic value of its position would have been enormous, and for precisely the same reason I can see why the Romans would have wanted to burn it. Their own city of Viroconium is down there somewhere, its grid pattern under the fields, all lines and squares and ruthlessly militarised efficiency. But I try not to think ill of the Romans. After all, they saved my friend Paul's life – if not his soul.

*

There are no friendships quite like the ones you make when you're thirteen, and I'm certain that the way me and Paul Felton knocked around together confused the hell out of our parents and teachers. I was bookish, nerdish, and about as sporty as a draught excluder. He was on the football team as often as he was in detention, driven by an inexhaustible anger at everyone and everything. His dad had died in the Falklands and his mum's new boyfriend was a shit, but that was all I knew. Yes, I said we were friends, but there are things that thirteen-year old boys just don't talk about. What drew us together were two things: *Doctor Who*, and the old Roman road that ran through the park behind his house.

I say 'park': Sutton Park was, and I suppose still is, nearly two and a half thousand acres of municipal recreation space for cyclers, joggers, and horse-riders. It has seven lakes, ancient woodlands which haven't been touched since the middle ages, and it preserves a one-and-a-half mile stretch of Roman road called Icknield Street which everywhere else is buried beneath concrete and tarmac, but in Sutton Park is hidden only beneath a thin skin of topsoil and grass. You could scratch away a few inches of dirt and stand on the same road that – with a bit of boyish imaginative license – carried legionnaires from the coasts of the Mediterranean up north to do battle with the marauding hordes of Pictish barbarians.

It fascinated us utterly. Paul and I had a pretty decent arrangement: he came around to mine to watch any episodes of *Doctor Who* that he might have missed due to things kicking off at home, and which I taped obsessively on our new VCR, in return for which I gained a certain amount of street cred for being friends with the school bad boy. We had a plan to save up our pocket money and buy a metal detector, absolutely confident that we'd find bits of armour, or gold coins or – best of all – rusted bits of weaponry lodged in old bone. But since Paul never got any money except the change he nicked when his mum sent him out for fags, and I was incapable of walking past a videogames arcade or a second-hand bookshop without spending every penny I had, it was slow going.

I think Paul must have finally lost patience with the plan, because late one evening he turned up at my place in a state of high excitement, covered in dirt and clutching something wrapped in a plastic carrier bag.

Mum opened the door to his knocking. 'Paul? It's very late, dear. Is everything…'

'Hi, Mrs Cooper!' he grinned, launching straight past her and upstairs to my room.

'Paul! Shoes!'

'Yeah I know! Brilliant, isn't it?'

I don't suppose she bothered to spare a moment's thought trying to work out what he meant by that, since teenage boys plainly occupied a parallel universe only marginally connected to the real world; just so long as she reminded herself to make me clear up the mud he left behind. Which she did. Rule number one in the Cooper household: *your guest, your mess.*

He barged in without knocking. I was in the middle of making an Airfix model of an X-wing, which was only slightly less embarrassing than some of the other things he could have caught me doing.

'Check this out!' he said, and tossed the carrier bag onto my desk.

'Yeah, hi, I'm fine thanks, how are you?' I scowled, and unwrapped it dubiously. Paul's finds were generally dangerous, often pornographic, occasionally illegal – and seldom safe to handle carelessly with bare hands. 'It's a shoe,' I observed, unimpressed.

To be precise it was a sandal, made of leather, a bit like

the kind worn by our Religious Ed teacher, Mr Holy-Molyneux.

'It's a Roman shoe,' he corrected.

'Are you shitting me?' Instantly this had become a million times cooler.

'I shit you not. It is a Roman legionnaire's *caliga*. I found it on the Street.' He didn't have to explain which street.

'But it looks like new.' I turned it over in my hands. I was no archaeologist – wasn't interested in any dates in History which had an AD after them – but I'd sort of expected leather which had been buried for two thousand years to be stiff and hard, or else disintegrating. This was neither. It was supple and shiny and – I gave it a sniff – yes, still stinky with Roman foot-sweat. Which, of course, it couldn't be.

'Bollocks,' was my considered opinion, and threw it back at him. 'This is a wind-up. Either you got this from a charity shop or you've been out mugging hippies.'

'It is not bollocks! It's from a real, genuine Roman foot-soldier. He was marching along, part of it snapped – see that bit there? So he chucked it away and put on a spare.'

'How can you possibly know that?'

Paul's eyes, usually dark and troubled, were on this occasion shining. 'Because I saw him.'

*

Such an outrageous claim demanded testing, and as an opportunity to completely take the piss out of him it couldn't be refused, because obviously there was no way it could be true. So it surprised me how readily he agreed that we should stake a look-out on Icknield Street the following night. It had to be at night, he said, not because they were ghosts – and he punched me so hard on the arm when I made a few harmless *woooooo!* noises that the bruise lasted for a week – but because something about other people being around caused interference. It did occur to me that he might have taken the latest episode of *Earthshock* a bit too seriously, but I didn't fancy another bruise so I kept my mouth shut. That, plus, as I say, the piss-take potential.

We found ourselves sitting in a large bush in the freezing cold on a March night, munching sweets and jumping like idiots at every sound. Paul had chosen a part of Sutton Park as far away from any lights as he could get – not that there were many. From our hiding place the remains of the Icknield Street agger was a flat, black ribbon seemingly hovering above the ground, while the trees around us were dim, rustling shadows against a sky the colour of orange charcoal. We saw several rabbits, something which might have been a fox, and shrank in terror at the approach of two human shapes, only to be disappointed when they stopped to kiss.

'Close-knit unit, are they?' I whispered at him, for which I earned another dead arm. 'Right, sod it,' I said. 'I'm off.'

'You can't go yet!' he protested.

I glared at him but I think the effect was lost in the dark. 'I am not spending the night sitting in the middle of a bush watching people snog!' I hissed back at him. 'It's pervy! Plus you keep hitting me!'

'Well you keep being a wanker, so sit down and shut up.'

I did as I was told, and we resumed our voyeuristic vigil.

When we finally heard the legion, it was a bit like when you go scanning through the airwaves on an old radio and you pick up the faint thread of human speech but it's gone before you can be sure you've even heard it, so you crawl back slowly with the tuning dial listening for coherence to emerge out of the crackle and hiss which is the background noise of the universe. Not that I suppose anyone these days knows what a radio is, let alone a tuning dial. Nevertheless, out of the rustling of wind and foliage emerged a faint rhythmic noise. Unsustained at first, only a random-sounding *one-and-two-and*, just enough to set my heart racing so hard that I was afraid I was hearing that and nothing else. Then came *a-three-and-a-four-and-a*, and while I was straining to hear more I realised that it had resolved clearly into the unmistakable sound of many dozens of footfalls. Marching.

Marching towards us.

I clutched Paul. 'What do we do?!'

'Shut up!' He forced me back down with his elbows in the small of my back. 'Lie still. Watch. Do not make a single. Fucking. Sound.'

I did exactly that. The noise grew louder, came abreast of us, and resolved into a dozen other combined sounds:

the creak of straps, the harshness of laboured breathing, muttered comments from one man to another, the heavy flap of their armour and the hollow clank of their gear. And the smell! A wide mantle of leather, sweat, wool, iron, piss, and spices swept after them, thick enough to insulate them from the cold on its own. If they were ghosts, then they were the most solid ghosts I had ever imagined. I could see nothing more of them than a bristling mass in the gloom. The tips of their javelins reflected dully the same burnt-orange colour of the city sky, and I knew then without a shadow of a doubt that they were real. If their weapons reflected the light of *our* sky then they were in *our* world; they weren't ghosts or illusions. The only other plausible explanation was that they were the result of too little sleep, too many sweets and too much *Doctor Who*, but I ask you, what thirteen-year old boy is going to side with plausibility over a park full of Roman legionnaires?

Paul and I managed to keep our cool until the last of them had disappeared into the greater darkness, and then we just lost it completely – whooping and yelling with excitement and jumping around madly so much that the locals in the houses bordering the park's edge could have been forgiven for thinking that an actual battle was being fought there. Then we made our separate ways home. Each of us got a bollocking from our folks, but it didn't make any difference; Paul was used to it and I was too wired to care.

It certainly didn't stop us from going back the

following night. And the next.

*

'How do you think they got here?' I whispered to Paul, as I peered out from our customary hiding place. 'Where do they go to?'

We were watching a group of half a dozen of them standing around a flaming brazier, cooking pieces of unidentified small mammal on sharp sticks and generally slobbing about in a way which we imagined was little different to soldiers of any time. A few others were off to one side, gambling with a pair of dice.

'*From* is hard to say,' he replied. 'These look like local auxiliaries, from their face tattoos. Probably Dobunni; they were generally a pretty Rome-friendly lot. *To* is easier. They'll be off up to the garrison at Viroconium to help keep the Welsh tribes from beating the crap out of each other. Or they could be really unlucky and get sent up to Hadrian's Wall to stop the Scots from beating the crap out of everybody else.'

It was incredible how much research he'd done off his own back. Our History teacher, Mr Perry, wouldn't have believed it. In fact, to use an obscenity fashionable at the time, old Pezza would have shit kittens if he'd known exactly how well-educated Paul was making himself.

But there was the thing: I was focussed on the mechanism of how their very existence in the park could be; they could have been Mayans or Daleks for all I cared, but Paul just bypassed those questions completely, accepted the mystery for what it was and ploughed headlong into it. I still can't make up my mind whether this was due to him having too much imagination or too little – either way, at the time I almost envied him his single-mindedness. I had too many real-world distractions to keep me grounded: school, Dad just having been made redundant, and even a cautiously burgeoning interest in Samantha Corey from the Third Form. Once the initial dazzle of Icknield Street's magic had faded, my mind needed to find some way of fitting its oddness with those other pieces of the whole puzzle for my place in the world to start making sense.

Take those soldiers chatting in the firelight, for example. Even though they were the only ones we could see, no way were they the only ones there. From their perspective the whole area must have been dotted with similar groups standing around similar fires. We knew this because every so often figures would come into view as they crossed the road, only to disappear on the other side like moths flying through a beam of torchlight. It was clear that something about the road was making them real; some interaction between its incredible age and our adolescent imaginations. Probably. Looking back on it now, I think it might have been fuelled by Paul's burning desire to escape his world whatever the cost.

'Heads up,' he pointed. 'Centurion's not happy.'

Below us the soldiers' commanding officer was berating them. Apparently, bivvying in the middle of the road itself was a Very Bad Thing, because he was ordering them to move using the sort of profanity that you didn't need an O-level in Latin to understand.

We watched them hurriedly gather their things together and disappear off to one side, and then Paul scared the hell out of me by breaking cover and scurrying towards where they'd been standing.

I was aghast. 'What are you *doing*?'

He paused long enough to grin back over his shoulder. 'Salvage!'

'But what if they catch you?'

He ignored me and crept closer.

Over the last few nights we'd managed to collect a few scraps and bits of rubbish left behind when the soldiers had gone, and just as with the shoe he'd first shown me, they remained in pretty good condition – although we discovered that the longer we waited before picking anything up, the quicker it succumbed to the accumulated weight of time. If we left it as late as the next morning, there was generally nothing left but what an archaeologist would have to dig up with a trowel. Plainly, Paul had decided he wanted something as fresh as possible.

I watched, terrified and unable to breathe, while he crept up onto the slight rise of the agger and swept his hands to and fro in the dark across the ground where the soldiers had been shooting the Roman equivalent of craps just a few minutes before. He obviously couldn't see too well; he kept stopping, picking up small bits of whatever, feeling them and then chucking them away. Every molecule of my trapped breath screamed at him to just get *out* of there, and then he waved something aloft triumphantly and came running back in a low crouch.

'Jackpot!' he announced, and fell into our bush laughing.

He'd found some coins. Three small, thin brass sestertes, missed as the soldiers had scraped together their belongings. He gave me one as payment for being lookout, he said, though I'd done nothing except kack myself – and kept the other two for himself, saying that he was going to find an expert who would tell him how much he could sell them for.

He didn't turn up to school the next day, or for several days after that. At the time I thought nothing of it, since his record for skiving was legendary, but when we next met at Icknield Street and I saw the state of him I knew that his disappearance had been down to something much less pleasant than playing hookey.

Both of his eyes were blackened and his lower lip was swollen and split open. He stood, wearing an oversized khaki jacket which he claimed to have belonged to his dead father but which I suspect came from an army surplus store, with his arms wrapped tightly about himself in a way that suggested physical pain.

'Jesus!' I said. 'What happened to you?'

He took a while to answer. He'd never talked about his home life before but I think deep down he knew we wouldn't be seeing each other again, and for the first time in his life he opened to me, or possibly anyone.

'Brian,' he spat. 'Mum's boyfriend. Fucking prick. You know I said I was going to find someone who could value those coins for us? Well I asked Mum, which was stupid.'

'Why?'

'Because she asked him, didn't she? Like, she couldn't tell that it was supposed to be just me-and-her business. So he finds out and he comes and accuses me of nicking them, doesn't he? I said where was I supposed to have nicked them from – a museum? Did I look like a bloody cat burglar? That got me this.' He pointed to one of his black eyes. 'I said I dug them out of the ground, dint I, and he said well you don't look much like fucking Indiana Jones either, and he gave me the other one.' His voice was thick and tight, as if he was trying to choke back anger, or tears, or both. I didn't know what to say. What response could I have made which wouldn't have sounded pathetically inadequate? Understand: there was no such thing as child-protection when we were kids. No Childline that you could call. If you went to the police with this sort of shit you were more likely to get a clip round the ear for wasting their time and taken straight back home where the pigs would nod understandingly about what an awkward troublemaking little sod you were, before leaving you to get a worse hiding than before.

No. There was nothing I could do. There was nothing Paul expected me to do, except one thing. He needed me on look-out one last time.

*

We lurked around the park until nightfall before finding our customary bush and settling in to wait for the legion.

It was raining, and our mood with each other was sour and tetchy.

'I don't see what good this will do,' I whispered to him. 'What's it going to prove? He'll still think you're a thief and a liar.'

'Fuck what he thinks,' Paul replied, with such cold and understated fury that it chilled my blood. 'It's not about that. I just need a thing, that's all.'

'What thing?'

But he refused to say.

This time when the legion marched past, with their armour glistening in the rain like the carapaces of beetles, a portion of the steeply banked agger crumbled away to the side, causing half a dozen soldiers to stumble sideways, cursing, and a lot of ill-natured jostling as the men behind tried to sidestep around the sudden pothole and shoved into their mates. Orders were shouted, the chaos resolved itself, and when the men had passed a small detail of engineers were left behind with two guards to effect a temporary repair. Working by the light of a single lantern, they set to with shovels and poles, ramming hardcore back into the hole while the guards watched them in that attitude of surly boredom which we'd come to find familiar. They'd dumped their packs and weapons in a heap at the side of the road while they huddled against the rain in their woollen cloaks, and from the way I felt Paul stiffen next to me I knew without having to be told what he was after.

'No!' I ordered, far more assertively than I'd ever

dared say anything to him. 'Paul, just no. This is insane.'
'A sword. A pilum. I don't care. Whatever's nearest. I'll
wave it in Brian's fat fucking face and see how he likes it.'
Rain and the moving shadows of foliage played across his
face, making it look like things were squirming under his
skin. 'I might see if he likes how it feels, too,' he added in
a dark whisper.

Before I could make a move to stop him, he'd gone.

Full credit to his sneakery: even I could barely see him,
and I knew he was there. The dark clothes in which he
was dressed must have been chosen deliberately for this,
and all that I could make out was the pale blur of his face
low to the ground as he crept like Gollum towards the
silhouettes of the soldiers.

Still, he could never have hoped to pull it off. It's
impossible for me even now, as a grown man – and
especially a civilian – to understand the kinds of instincts
which seasoned soldiers develop to keep themselves
alive. Something in the animal hindbrain must wake up.
Something which can detect the scent or air displacement
of another human body, or the subtle change in the timbre
of the sound of rain as it falls around a human form. I
don't know what made that soldier turn around and look
straight at Paul just as he was reaching for the nearest
pack. Maybe it was just dumb bad luck.

Paul froze, the worst possible thing he could have
done, because the legionnaire didn't. Freezing in surprise
can kill a man – or a boy. The legionnaire gave a cry of
alarm and darted forward, grabbing Paul by his

outstretched arm.

Don't ask why it suddenly occurred to me that this was a clever thing to do, but at this point I decided that I needed to rescue my friend, so I leapt out of hiding and ran yelling for the scene, just as the other Romans were turning in surprise. I managed to grab Paul's ankle as the legionnaire was pulling him up onto the agger, and for a moment my friend was caught in a bizarre tug-of-war between us.

The soldier's eyes locked with mine. I saw that they were brown, wide with bafflement at seeing me, and the sudden shock of his awareness communicated itself like electricity through Paul's body. What had those eyes witnessed – what scenes of an ancient world two thousand years lost to me and now just green mounds in the grass, but to him an everyday walking, talking reality? I was within touching distance of a mystery which felt like it might throw open the vaults of my soul, or destroy me utterly. The only time I've ever felt anything close to that was the first time I had sex – and here, now, sitting on top of the Wrekin, waiting for the Cornovii to arrive.

Then, with a sudden savage tug, Paul was gone, grabbed in a vicious headlock and rammed full body into the mud of the road, screaming my name.

One of the other soldiers had snatched up a pilum from the bundle of packs and had his arm cocked towards me. I watched rain drip from the weapon's pyramidal iron point, fascinated.

'Gaz, help me!' screamed Paul, though his mouth was

muffled by the ground. 'Help me! For God's sake, *please!*'
I mean come on – what did he expect me to do? Really?
I ran.

Just not quite fast enough.

At first I thought I'd tripped over something in the
dark, because I pitched forward suddenly and nearly
went headlong. Then I thought I must have snagged my
foot on a root or a plastic bag or something, because my
right leg was fighting some heavy resistance. A second
later, when the pain began to burn in the back of my
thigh, I figured it was a cramp; it wasn't until I reached
back and felt the metal javelin-head hanging out of my
flesh and its wooden shaft dragging along the ground
behind me like an obscene tail that I realised what had
happened.

In retrospect I was incredibly lucky. If that legionnaire
hadn't been snap-throwing hastily, in the dark and the
rain, the pilum would at the very least have skewered my
leg completely, if not hit me in the torso and killed me
outright. As it was, I was able to yank it out in panic and
stumble a few more yards until shock dropped me like a
sack of bricks. From that position, all I could do was
watch numbly as the soldier who had hit me drew a short
sword and stepped off the road towards me to finish the
job.

He actually made it several yards past the road's ditch
– further than we'd ever seen any of them come – before
he stopped, looking around in puzzlement. I thought that
maybe he'd come far enough to see something of our

world: streetlights, perhaps, or maybe just the orange glow of the city sky, and wondered what great conflagration awaited him and his company beyond the night-time horizon. Then his face creased in pain and he screamed. Thankfully, darkness hid from my sight the full horror of what happened to him next, as two thousand years of cheated time fell on him in a few seconds, but for a moment I saw the agonised confusion of a young man who suddenly found himself to be a sallow and withered geriatric, before the flesh turned cadaverous and rotted from bones which themselves crumbled to powder. The leather bindings of his armour dissolved, its pieces blooming with rust even as they fell, and where they landed the ground swallowed them as if he had never existed at all.

*

A month after my grounding for having been idiotic enough to go climbing trees in the dark and falling onto some spiked railings, as my story went, I returned in broad, safe daylight with a trowel and a dug around the area where I thought I'd been hit – to prove to myself that it had really happened – as if the scar and the limp weren't enough – but I never found anything.

*

It was around ten years later, when I was in the final year of a post-grad course, that I came home to my bedsit one afternoon to find the door smashed open.

Worried that the burglar might still be inside, I edged in cautiously, but needn't have bothered; he'd probably heard me the moment I'd come through the front door two floors below.

'Gaz, mate, don't be afraid, it's me, Paul,' called a gruff voice.

I found him sprawled at the table in my little galley kitchen, with the fridge door wide open and most of its contents on the way towards disappearing into his stomach. On the floor under the table was a large knapsack and a pair of hunting spears, and I saw an army -issue gladius at his side. He looked like life had been treating him harshly, and that he was thriving on it. He was huge enough to begin with, but his size was exaggerated by layers of leather, animal skins, and coarsely-woven fabric. The smell which came from him prowled the room like a beast. It was campfire smoke and the mud of long moorland marches with hard fighting at the end; it was ocean salt and tar and the perfume of sailors' whores; it was everything in between, a lifetime of adventuring. But his hair was neatly cropped and he was clean-shaven in the Roman style, and from his tanned and scarred face gleamed the bright blue eyes of my childhood friend. The boy who had loved *Doctor Who* and hated Geography lessons.

'How did you find me?' I asked.

'Your mum's still in the old place,' he replied. His voice was thickly accented; still Brummy, but in a way I'd never heard before. 'I was sorry to hear about your father.'

I shook that one aside for a much more important

question. 'Where have you *been*?'

'Everywhere!' he laughed. 'The road goes everywhere, old friend, and it took me with it. I joined up, can you believe that? I enlisted! They didn't want me at first, but I made myself useful, learned the language, learned how to look after their horses and their weapons.' He laughed again. 'Can you imagine the look on old Perry's face if he knew my Latin was now better than his?'

He chuckled at the thought and then subsided into a brooding silence. I didn't know what he was expecting of me. We were so alien to each other, it seemed impossible that there was anything we could chat about. The weather? Football? There was, in fact, only one meaningful thing I could say to him.

'Paul, the day you … left, I'm sorry I couldn't…'

'None of that,' he cut me off. 'Just don't. There was nothing you could have done. Leave it.'

'So are you back then? For good, I mean?'

'Gods, no. This place is diseased. I've seen it a few times, passing by – you'd be surprised at now many thin places there are in the skin of the world, by the way – but I've never been tempted.'

'Then why?'

'I've got my papers. The Empire's pulling out of this island and things are going to get nasty in the next few years, so I'm off up into Wales to find myself a nice strong place with some land and a few people I can trust. I came to see if you wanted to be one of them.'

It was my turn to laugh. 'Me? I'd be bugger all use as a

farmer and even worse as a fighter.'

Paul leaned forward, his face eager. 'Oh, but you *know* things. There are always going to be strong arms; what we're going to be missing is strong heads. You were always the clever one. You can give us knowledge, make us stronger, help us survive what's coming. What do you say?'

'I don't know…'

'Because what can you do in this place?' He gestured around my bedsit in evident contempt. 'What good can you do here except fill another desk and pay more tax until they let you die, another grey old man in a grey old country? Come to mine! It's green, and red with blood, and alive!' He slammed the table, making everything jump, including me. There was fire in his eyes, and what I had at first taken to be the warmth of friendship I saw now was the shine of battle. I was nothing more to him than an asset to be seized, a resource to be plundered like the contents of my fridge, and I felt genuine fear that his politeness had been just for old times' sake – he would simply refuse to take no for an answer and drag me off to his feral time, or else slay me where I stood for my defiance. I think he saw that in my expression – some reflection of what he had become staring back at him, because he subsided with a rueful chuckle.

'Ah well,' he said. 'I had to try. Can't blame a man for asking.' He stood, gathered his things together, and paused at the door. 'Have a good life, Gareth. Try not to regret too much.'

Paul left, and I never saw him again.

*

Up here on the Wrekin it's now completely deserted. For the moment. Every now and then I fancy I can hear a snatch of singing or child's laughter, and that is most definitely peat smoke I can smell.

Paul might not have persuaded me to spend my future in his past, but he did inadvertently set my life on the road which it has followed for the past forty years. What he said about the number of thin places in the skin of the world was quite true. I know; I've spent my life investigating them – everything from Mayan pyramids and the Nazca lines to stone circles, primeval forest glades, and even remnants of the old Birmingham back-to -backs which most people think have all been demolished – but the more of these ancient mysteries I've seen, the less I've been able to solve the greatest and most ancient of them all. The one called simply 'if'.

If I hadn't taken that job.

If I'd married that woman.

If I'd only chosen the road.

I look down from this ancient height to the Shropshire plain sprawled with the lights of towns and villages which one day will be nothing more than green mounds in the grass, but which at the moment are full of people enjoying the bright now of their lives and ignoring the wide darkness of time surrounding them on all sides, and I recall the look of terror on that Roman soldier's face as he found himself in an alien time, and I wonder how often that same look has been on my own face in recent years. The expression of a young man realising that he has become suddenly and inexplicably old.

And here they are come to meet me, out of the warm-orange doorways set below thatched conical roofs, with gold gleaming about their throats and smiles on their faces and songs in the voices. The Cornovii have come for me, and I am home.

Mob Rule

'Jesus, will you look at that,' said Sean, pointing with his bottle towards the dance floor.

Jase looked, and nearly choked on his Stella.

The bloke out there, dancing right in the middle, looked like a reject from *Little Britain*. Above spindly legs in skinny-fit jeans, his massive belly defied both gravity and the integrity of his own shirt-buttons as he leapt around waving his arms like a man trying to ward off a swarm of killer bees. But that wasn't the thing which inspired Jase's awestruck horror. Neither was it his clenched, perspiring face and the eye-wateringly ugly orange-yellow wig which flapped up and down on his head. It was the two blondes dancing with him. They had to be the most gorgeous creatures Jase had ever set eyes on.

'That is ... just...' he managed, '...so *wrong.*'

Sean swigged his beer in grim agreement.

At first Jase thought the blondes were taking the piss, that they were dancing around the guy ironically, just to rub his face in the fact that he stood no chance. Lord knew, it was the kind of treatment someone like him or Sean would get. But the more he watched the more he became convinced that they were genuinely into it.

'What was that you were saying?'

Jenny and Trish were back from the ladies.

Jase gave Jenny the beer he'd bought for her while Trish draped herself across Sean's shoulders and planted a bright red lipstick kiss on his cheek.

'We're just checking out Saturday Night Fever over there,' he said.

Jenny looked, and laughed. 'You cruel buggers. Leave him alone; he looks like he's just enjoying himself, that's all. Which is what you should be doing, by the way, not making fun of people. Happy birthday, boys.'

'Birthday!' shouted Sean.

'Happy birthday to us!' echoed Jase. 'God bless us and all who sail in us!'

Born only four days apart at the end of March, they'd lived in the same street as each other, gone to the same school, and celebrated their birthdays together for as long as either of them could remember. It was a standing joke that spring didn't officially begin until they did. People who met them for the first time assumed that they were twins – the non-identical sort – and even though they weren't, Sean still liked to pretend that he had the authority of an elder brother, seeing as how he'd beaten Jase into the world by a whole ninety-six hours. Jase, for the most part, was happy to let this state of affairs be.

'How would you be if I got myself a big old belly full of enjoying myself like that, then?' Jase teased, pushing out his stomach and jiggling what there was of it like Father Christmas.

'You never would,' she said. 'You're too bloody vain, you are.'

She may have had a point there. Still, he didn't see why he shouldn't be proud of his six-pack; he'd worked hard for it. To disguise how close to the mark she was, he grabbed her around the waist and buried his face in her cleavage, snorting and making her shriek with laughter.

'Well I think it's sweet,' said Trish.

'It's not sweet,' hmphed Sean. It's revolting.'

'What's wrong with a middle-aged man in a nightclub?'

'Oh, and you'd get off with him, would you?'

'I never said that!'

Jase threw a crisp at him. 'You're just jealous because that old fart has copped off with a couple of girls who are so far out of your league you'd need a megaphone to chat them up.'

'What's he on about?' demanded Trish, swatting Sean. 'What does he mean "out of your league"? Don't you think I'm as pretty as them girls?'

'Why are you hitting me? I didn't bloody say anything!'

'Someone better call the retirement home,' Jenny interrupted. 'I think the disco king has had enough.'

It seemed she was right. The hideously bewigged man was staggering from the dance floor with an arm draped around each of the blondes.

'Still,' she added, 'I suppose it's nice to see someone caring for the older generation.'

'They're going to do more than care for him,' realised Sean in horror, as the trio weaved its way through the press of clubbers.

'He's not...' said Jenny.

'He can't be...' said Trish.

'He only fucking is!' Jase punched the air and whooped in triumph. 'He's taking two for the team! Get in there, granddad!'

It was just a little bit too loud, even by nightclub standards. The man turned, saw, changed tack and angled his armfuls of bimbo towards them.

'Birthday party, is it?' he asked.

'We are thirty-eight today,' announced Sean, saluting the man with his beer bottle. 'Nice hair-piece, by the way.' Trish giggled.

The man didn't reply. His gaze was lazy, ranging over the four of them in a not entirely friendly manner. He was a lot larger than he had seemed out on the dance floor, too; his paunch more the spread of a once-muscular man gone to seed than simply the poor fitness of a suburban drone. He seemed to be calculating something, and was apparently pleased by the result, because he gave scornful laugh and turned away from them again, steering his two dancing partners back towards the door.

'What was that all about?' asked Jase.

Jenny shrugged. 'Who cares?'

'I care.' Sean was staring hard after the man's retreating back as if he could burn holes between his shoulder blades. 'And I'm going to find out.' He stood up, shoving his chair aside, but Trish put a restraining hand on his arm.

'Leave it babe. He's just a sad, pathetic loser. Don't let him ruin your birthday.'

Sean subsided, and they didn't see the old man in the hideous wig for the rest of the night, but a shadow had been cast over their evening, nevertheless.

*

Things took a turn for the weird three days later when the man turned up as a customer at the post-office window next to the one which Jase was working. At first he didn't recognise the guy; without the Toupee of Doom he was just another fat, balding, middle-aged businessman buying Euros for a trip abroad. Fortunately he didn't seem to have recognised Jase either, serving at the next window along and watching him like a hawk – as if this chunky Casanova was likely to start busting some moves amongst the padded envelopes and then shag Margaret from window number three in the photo booth.

But he did nothing in the slightest bit eccentric. He was polite and quietly spoken, chatting with Vicky on the Bureau de Change counter about how he was travelling to Greece on business. What business was it? Oh, nothing very exciting – he imported olives and various other Mediterranean snack-foods for wholesale to restaurants and market traders. Really? How interesting; it must have been nice having a job which took him abroad like that. Well, it paid the bills, didn't it?

Eavesdropping on this terminally bland banter, Jase

thought he preferred it when the guy was being a dick.

When he'd left with his wallet full of Monopoly money and Vicky's attention was momentarily elsewhere, Jase sneaked a look at the payment details. The man's name was Robert Cheevers. With minimal extra lurking around on the internet Jase was able to find out that he did indeed run a small food import company called Colchis Foods. There was no reason to suspect that he'd been lying – and if asked, Jase wouldn't have been able to say why he was so interested in the man, beyond the massive discrepancy between how he'd acted in the club and what he was like in the broad light of day. It was almost enough to make him wonder if the man was hiding anything, even though none of it was in the slightest bit his business.

However, it became very much his business the following weekend, when Sean ended up in hospital.

*

That Friday it was half-price entry to Bernie's for single ladies, so Jenny and Trish went ahead of the boys with the intention of meeting them at the bar. Jase and Sean took some time locating their girlfriends in the heaving press of clubbers, with the lights strobing everywhere and the music so loud they could barely hear themselves shouting to each other, but Jase didn't need Sean to say anything for him to realise something was very wrong. He had snapped to a stiff-necked halt and was glaring at the crowd ranged along the bar.

'Who you eye-olating now?' Jase laughed, and then he saw. 'Oh shit.'

Robert Cheevers, one-man disco army, was standing with his wig resplendent in the flashing lights, drinking and laughing with Trish.

Jase's reflexes were a fraction too slow for him to stop Sean from charging over there.

'What the fuck are you doing talking to him?' Sean demanded. 'What the *actual* fuck?'

'Get off!' she complained. 'We're just having a chat, that's all.'

'Where's Jenny?' asked Jase, but nobody was paying him any attention.

'Steady now, mate,' said Cheevers, rising, palms outward and placatory, but with a strange smile on his face which belied them.

Sean slapped them away. 'You're nobody's fucking mate here, *mate*. Got that?'

'Sean...' Jase tried to butt in. He didn't like the way the sinews were standing out on his friend's neck, or the flush of rage which was rising into his face.

Cheevers' smile widened. 'I remember you two now – you're the birthday boys, aren't you?'

'What the fuck's that got to do with anything?'

The older man just laughed at them. It was a drawling, arrogant sound, and for a moment Jase was seized with the delicious fantasy of choking it back down the old fart's throat. It was utterly unlike him, and a very different kind of fear began to twitch and uncoil in his stomach. What was happening here?

Jenny appeared from the crowd. 'What's going on?'

'Where have you been?' he asked, a little more harshly than he'd intended.

Her expression turned frosty. 'Having a chat with some of the girls from work, if that's okay with you, *dear*.'

'Sorry, look, I didn't mean...'

But Sean interrupted him. 'And you left Trish alone with this scumbag?'

'Oi! First thing, I'm not her mother, okay? Second...'

'Sean!' protested Trish. 'Just leave it, will you?'

'Yes Sean,' echoed Cheevers, smirking. 'Leave it, why don't you? Go on, sheep boys. Pair of Aries fairies. Follow Bo-Peep here like good little lambs and find a friendly farmer to fuck you.'

Trish giggled. Jase groaned. Up to that point the situation could have been rescued – it was just a bit of shouting, no harm done, they'd all heard worse – but the moment this wanker made Trish giggle at her boyfriend's expense, well. That was it, folks. Everybody out of the pool.

With a roar, Sean was on him. Or at least, would have been on him if Cheevers hadn't sidestepped with an agility which seemed odd for a man who looked so ungainly, and as Sean hurtled past followed him around with a shove in the small of the back which sent him crashing into the next couple at the bar. Glass broke, beer spilled, voices yelled.

'Sean the Sheep,' mocked Cheevers. 'Headstrong and stupid, just like every one of your kind.'

Jase could hear Jenny yelling at him to leave it out,

walk away, don't do this, but her voice was indistinct, as if muffled by the thick layer of wool which was wadded tightly in his skull. It crushed out rational thought and heated his brain into a sweating, throbbing mass, and the only thing that seemed to release the pressure was by jumping in to help his friend beat the shit out of the smirking bastard in front of them.

After that, things got a bit confusing.

*

Clarity returned in a blast of chilly night air on the pavement outside Bernie's, which was where the Romanian bouncers threw Jase and Sean. Having been the victim of, as they saw it, a two-on-one attack, Cheevers had been allowed to remain inside. As were the girls. When Sean had said 'So are you two coming with us then?', which had been no mean feat considering that his head was wedged in a bouncer's armpit at the time, Trish had just glared at him and asked him if he thought he was being funny.

Complaining that all of this was grossly unfair on the grounds that they'd seen other fights broken up with everybody involved being thrown out regardless of who started it, didn't help. Mr Cheevers, they were told, was a friend of the management.

Now, sitting outside the club with a pair of East European door-gorillas giving them filthy looks, Sean rubbed his sore neck and asked Jase: 'Did you find that funny? Because I bloody didn't.'

'Don't talk to me,' groaned Jase.

'Listen man...'

'I said don't fucking talk to me, alright?!'

In the meantime Jenny was trying to convince Trish to leave with her.

'Why have I got to leave just because Sean was being a wanker?' she sulked, and took a swig from her bottle of WKD.

'Yes, Jenny,' added Cheevers. 'Why?' He was sporting the start of a black eye and his ridiculous wig was slightly askew, but he seemed otherwise none the worse for wear. If anything, he was perkier than ever.

'Excuse me,' Jenny replied. 'No offence? But I don't know you from Adam. I'm talking to my friend.' Then she noticed the bottle that Trish was drinking from. 'Did he buy that?'

Trish frowned at it. 'I can't remember.'

Jenny took the bottle off her, plonked it on the table and grasped her by the wrist. 'Come on,' she ordered. 'We're going with the boys.'

'But why?' Trish whinged.

'Because I'm not going to watch one of my friends get Rohypnolled by some loser with a dead cat on his head, that's why.'

Outside, Jase was having less success with Sean, who had decided that he was going to wait until Cheevers came out ('and then make him eat that fucking horrible rug', were his exact words), and wasn't being persuaded otherwise.

Jase couldn't believe what he was hearing. 'Will you

listen to yourself? You sound like something out of a crap Guy Ritchie film. What the hell is wrong with you? Picking fights in a nightclub? How did you get so fucking gangsta all of a sudden?'

'Look, are you going to back me up or not?'

'No! Of course I'm not going to "back you up"! You're acting like a dick! Sean, mate, listen, I'll follow you anywhere. Remember that time at Spaghetti Junction, all that scaffolding? I broke my arm in two places, remember? I'll go to the ends of the earth with you, you know that, but this? You're talking about assaulting some old bloke in an alleyway!'

'Gonna do more than fucking assault him,' Sean muttered darkly.

That fear in Jase's stomach uncoiled a bit further, making him feel sick. 'Well then I'm sorry, mate,' he said. 'You're on your own there. I'm not getting mixed up in that.'

Sean's determination to do Cheevers some serious injury didn't falter in the slightest when Jenny brought out Trish, who was staggering and looking quite glazed.

'You don't want to see your girlfriend safely home, then?' Jenny asked him acidly.

'Since Jase is being such a pussy I imagine the two of you can do a decent job of that,' he returned. 'I've got some unfinished business to take care of.'

'Come on. Let's leave Charles bloody Bronson to it.' Jase led her away, with Trish trailing. 'When they were safely out of earshot, he added 'I don't know what's got into him. I've never seen him like this before.'

'Do you know what?' she replied. 'I really don't give a toss. Let's just find a taxi.'

*

Sean smoked his way through a packet of fags while he waited, hoping that Cheevers would only stick around long enough to pull, and that he wouldn't be forced to wait in the freezing cold until the early hours. He was angry, yes – more pissed off than he could remember having been at anything for a long time – but he didn't think it would stand up to a case of hypothermia too well.

He was rewarded when, a little after eleven, Cheevers left with his arm draped around the shoulders of a gorgeous Asian girl. How did he do it? That was what Sean wanted to know. How was it so fucking easy for him? Did he drug them? Or was he just enormously well hung? He felt an uncontrollable bitterness and resentment surge outwards from the pit of his belly like lava, burning his limbs and propelling him after the pair as they turned down an alley by the side of the club. This wasn't about Trish; it never had been. Not really.

By the time he caught up to them, Cheevers already had his hand up the girl's skirt – what little there was of it – and was too preoccupied to prevent Sean from grabbing him by the scruff of his shirt and flinging him across the alley where he crashed into the opposite wall. His wig flapped from one side of his head. That thing, Sean thought, if nothing else he'd see that Godawful hairpiece trampled into the mud.

Cheevers got to his feet, dusting his hands off and grinning, which was not at all the reaction Sean had been expecting. His teeth were very large and crooked. It might have been the poor light, but there seemed to be something peculiar about his eyes, too.

'So,' Cheevers said, 'the young male finally plucks up courage to challenge the elder for dominance.'

'Whatever, you fucking nut-job. I'm here to teach you what happens when you mess with my girl.'

Cheevers shrugged. 'Same thing. Come on then, Rambo.' He moved towards Sean, and as the streetlight shifted on his face Sean saw what was so very wrong with his eyes. The pupils were rectangular slots, slightly narrower in the middle, like hourglasses lying on their sides. 'Rambo! Get it?' he leered, snaggle-toothed and drooling. 'See what I did there?'

Sean was so utterly astonished by this – too truly amazed to be frightened, which was a shame, because fear might have saved him – that he let Cheevers get close enough to head-butt him so suddenly and savagely that the force of it not only fractured the front of his skull but drove the back of it against the wall in a sickening flat crunch.

The girl was screaming before his body hit the ground.

'Less of that,' growled Cheevers. 'You were about to render unto Caesar that which is Caesar's, remember? So. Get on your knees and get rendering.'

*

Jase wasn't an idiot. The first thing he did after visiting

Sean in hospital was call the police. That was, of course, after getting over the shock of seeing his friend lying heavily bandaged in an intensive care ward with tubes and wires plugged into him everywhere. There was more life in the monitors around him than in the broken machine of his body. The doctors had put him in a chemical coma to stop his brain from swelling so much that it killed him. His face was the colour of bruised candles.

The bastard had cut him as well. Used a broken bottle or something to carve a strange shape like a seven with a tail curved over itself into his forehead. That made it worse, somehow. It hadn't been done in the red mist of a brawl, but afterwards, as Sean had been lying unconscious and probably dying in the alleyway's filth. It was a gesture of absolute power over, and complete contempt for, another human being, and even if it hadn't happened to Jase's friend it would still have enraged him. His own face burned with shame.

'I should have done something,' he said, his voice thick.

Jenny tightened her grip on his arm. 'Babe, you weren't even there.'

'That's the point. If I'd stayed there I could've stopped him from making an idiot of himself, just like you stopped Trish.'

She turned his face towards her. 'Listen to me. If you'd stayed, you'd probably be either lying there with him, or in a police cell. I know it sounds heartless but leaving him was the smartest thing you could've done.'

'Heartless? Just a bit! He is right there, you know.'

'Jase, you've been following Sean all your life. He's been calling the shots and you've been tagging along after him and it's only a miracle that something serious like this hasn't happened before now. You acted like an adult human male for once, and not some kind of pack animal. You can't blame yourself for that.'

'No. I know exactly who to blame.' He gestured helplessly at the wound on his friend's brow. 'I mean what kind of person *does* that?'

Jenny peered closer at it. 'A Capricorn,' she said.

Jase blinked. 'What?'

'It's a symbol for Capricorn. Don't you ever read your horoscope?'

He snorted. 'Load of bollocks.'

'Not to the person who did this,' she pointed out.

'But Sean isn't a Capricorn. He's an Aries. We both are...' Jase stopped. 'The bastard,' he whispered.

'What?'

'He called us "sheep-boys". It's a stamp. A tag. Cheevers has marked Sean as his property.' He laughed humourlessly. 'Sean's been astrologically owned.'

So Jase told the police everything about the fight in the club and about Sean's intentions afterwards. They in turn promised to send someone to ask Mr Cheevers a few questions.

After that, he heard precisely nothing. Nobody got back to him about it. Nobody responded to any of his follow-up calls beyond saying that they couldn't comment on the progress of an ongoing investigation. Jase began to doubt that there even *was* an ongoing investigation. It wouldn't have surprised him to find that the police had gone out there, had a nice friendly chat with Mr Cheevers because he was a 'friend of the management', slapped each other on the backs and then filed the whole thing under B for bullshit.

It didn't seem possible that a man as softly-mannered as the Cheevers who had bought Euros in his post office earlier in the week was capable of such violence. *But of course, he wasn't wearing his wig then,* he thought, and wondered how that even made sense.

He went to see the alley – why, he wasn't sure. It wasn't likely that he'd find anything that the police had missed, but then maybe they only did those really detailed fingertip searches when there was a murder involved. It seemed ridiculous that he could find anything.

And yet there it was.

At head height, stuck to the bricks: a tuft of yellow fake hair. Sean had obviously got Cheevers up against this wall at some point, probably before his bouncer mates had waded in. Jase looked at the tuft more closely, and found that it wasn't very much like human hair at all, even for a wig. It glistened like a Brillo pad made of gold, and it was altogether too fluffy – more like wool. He rolled it thoughtfully between his thumb and forefinger, and found his skin tingling unpleasantly.

Instantly, every instinct screamed at him to find this man and punish him, never mind his connections or how strong he was. His mind flooded with fantasies of violence: Cheevers bleeding underfoot, broken, weeping, dead. He tried to squash it down; that kind of thinking hadn't done Sean any good. But it was hard. His head was stuffed and sweating again and his mouth was full of the metallic taste of adrenalin.

Absently, he pushed the scrap of wool into his jeans pocket, and the feeling faded immediately.

That worm of fear in his stomach was fully awake now and squirming. There was something terribly wrong going on here, and it had taken an interest in his friends.

Jase decided he needed to know as much as he could about Cheevers and what the hell he was carrying around on his head if he was going to do anything about it – and certainly before he got anywhere near Cheevers again.

*

He Googled the man. He started with everything publicly available about his business, Colchis Foods, which was precious little and nothing he couldn't have guessed anyway, so he ditched such traditional methods of information gathering and turned to his social networks. He flicked through his friends' feeds, and then his friends' friends, and *their* friends' friends in a great outward branching on Facebook, Twitter, Tumblr, Instagram – anything, looking for photographs or gossip about Cheevers. Jase joined circles, conversations and lists; noting names, collecting numbers, making contacts, and in the process he heard from dozens people – mostly young women, but quite a few of their partners too – stories of how they'd been, well, not quite raped exactly, but you couldn't call what had happened to them entirely consensual either.

Yet nobody had reported him, and no arrest had been made. What gave a man that kind of power, he wondered.

And then, at a point so early in the morning that his eyes felt like two sandblasted ping-pong balls bulging from their sockets, he found the one photograph that unlocked everything for him.

It looked at first like just another one in dozens of forgettable nightclub scenes: grinning faces squashed too close together, gurning at the camera, over-exposed and fuzzy – except that the figure in the middle was definitely Cheevers with his arms around two predictably stoned-looking girls. Their pupils were bright with red-eye, but Cheevers must have been wearing some kind of weird contacts because his eyes were glowing white-green and rectangular, exactly like a goat's eyes.

Jase enjoyed himself for a few minutes with a simple photo-editing app and drew an Aries sign on Cheevers' forehead, then sent it back out into the world. *See how you like it*, he thought, with childish satisfaction.

And still that bloody toupee blazed gold in the camera flash. Jase could see now that it didn't look remotely like human hair at all – how could he have missed it? – but exactly like wool.

Or fleece.

'No', he whispered at the screen. 'No. Fucking. Way.'

With trembling fingers he Googled *golden* and *fleece* and *Colchis*, and settled back to watch the world he thought he knew reassemble itself in strange and marvellous new shapes.

*

That Friday night in Bernie's, Jase made sure he was sitting in the most obvious, open space he could find. It was well he did, because when Cheevers stormed into the club he plainly wasn't in a partying frame of mind. The bouncers stood by nervously as he marched over to the bar and lifted Jase clear off his seat by the front of his shirt so that his feet dangled six inches off the floor.

Even though he'd been expecting trouble, it still came as a shock. The strength in this tubby little man's body was monstrous, as was the expression on his face. It was bright red, with oblong eyes slitted in rage and his nostrils flaring as he bellowed into Jase's face.

'*You'd challenge me, would you?!*'

This close, Jase could see that wig for the fleece that it was. Golden, but not the colour of treasure. This was the diseased yellow of jaundice, of suppurating wounds, of colostomy bags on cancer wards, and it stank with the musk of a rutting animal long past its prime.

'Easy there tiger,' he choked. 'I thought you were a lover, not a fighter.'

Cheevers shook him until his jaw rattled like castanets. 'Fucking sheep!' he snarled. 'I'll make what happened to your friend look like a fucking holiday camp! There won't be a piece of you big enough to piss on!'

'Bit of a public place for a kicking like that,' Jase gasped. It really was getting quite hard to breathe.

Cheevers grinned. He had no upper teeth left, just a wide bony gum, and his lower incisors were long and yellowed. They looked like the kind of teeth which might chew through human flesh just as happily as tin cans or tyres. 'And you think that will protect you,' he sneered. 'You know nothing, sheep boy.'

'I know that wherever you found that,' Jase nodded at the fleece, 'it doesn't belong to you. It's of Aries, and you're nothing but a thief.'

'This! Place! Is! Mine!' Cheevers shouted, shaking him again. 'Everything in it! Is mine! Your women! Are mine! I will sire my get upon them while you watch like the ball-less cowards you are!' And he drew his head back to strike.

'I think they might have something to say about that,' put in a quiet voice. It was Jenny, and beside her, Trish. Behind them was a score of other women, many of whom were Jase's new friends – all of whom, including their friends, partners, brothers, and everybody *they* knew, had been invited by him here tonight.

'I thought you said something about pack animals,' he said to her.

'Not tonight.' Her voice was low, and full of loathing as she stared with naked hostility at Cheevers. 'Not for *that*.'

Jase could see the dawning realisation on Cheevers'

face that what he had taken to be a crowd of nervous bystanders were neither nervous, nor idly standing by. Most were on their feet and standing a lot closer than they had been a few moments ago. The strength went out of his arms, and he lowered Jase to the floor.

'This isn't about being a sheep,' Jase explained to the twitching goat-creature which was trying to look in every direction at once. 'Or a follower. Not any more. Aries is a *ram.*'

'And this is your flock! Cowards and weaklings with nothing in their heads other than to dance and rut themselves into oblivion!' It laughed at him, a great bray of scorn, but Jase thought he could hear a ragged edge of fear in it and his blood ran hot at the sound.

'Yeah, I know, but what can you do? They're still going to wipe the floor with you.'

It threw itself at him, raging incoherently, but dozens of hands came to his rescue, and dragged the spitting, bucking creature into the middle of the dance floor. They tore the golden fleece from its head and instantly he was once again nothing more than a fat, middle-aged man, trembling and snot-faced with terror.

'Wait!' he pleaded. 'Please! We can talk about this!'

Jase accepted the fleece from his people and turned the hateful thing over in his hands critically. It had no such power over him – or at least, none that was not already in him. He felt that power now, reaching out into the crowd around him, binding them to him and each other, making them his. But not entirely – not yet. There was one thing left which needed to be done.

He looked at Cheevers. 'No we can't,' he said. 'This thing,' he held the fleece up, 'wherever you found it, isn't the reason. It just amplifies what's already there. You did what you did because it was already in you, and for that you're going to have to pay. By the way,' he added. 'You called us a "flock" earlier, but flock is for birds. Do you know what a group of sheep is really called?'

Cheevers screamed his defiance and despair.

'We're called a mob.'

And Jason watched with lordly satisfaction as his mob tore their enemy apart.

The Gas Street Octopus

This is a true story. It was told to me by a friend of the guy that died.

Everybody's heard that New York has alligators in the sewers – that's probably not true. You might have heard that Birmingham has more canals than Venice – that definitely *is* true. We can go one better than the Big Apple, because we've got man-eating octopuses in the canals.

Nobody knows for sure how they got there. Most likely some escaped from the Sea Life Centre at Brindley Place, because octopuses are highly intelligent and notorious escape artists. There are many stories of them leaving their tanks at night to raid and eat the inhabitants of other tanks. Give them a hole wider than their beak and woosh – gone. But it also means that they can creep up into places you'd never expect, like the grey water drainage pipes and sewage systems of canal-side properties, for example.

So this friend of a friend – let's call him Gary – lived alone in a swanky apartment overlooking Gas Street Basin, with a balcony and a water view, and one night after having some mates around for a few beers he woke up in the early hours needing to answer a call of nature. He went into the bathroom and lifted up the lid and got on with things, still half-asleep and not really looking because, as we all know, blokes tend to aim only vaguely in the right direction. But then he heard something splashing heavily in the bowl, and he looked down.

And there's this octopus. Looking at him. And right away, he could tell that the creature wasn't happy.

From the octopus' point of view, it must have thought it was being attacked by a rival male – which in a sense it was – and so, backed into a corner and being 'inked over' by an admittedly fairly short tentacular appendage, it quite understandably retaliated, launching itself at its opponent. Octopuses are capable of short bursts of incredible speed when on the attack and Gary, still half-asleep, simply wasn't quick enough.

Now, it would be a lie to say that, to begin with and for the briefest of moments, the sensation of having an octopus latched on to his groin was not entirely unpleasant. They are, after all, mostly muscle. But they also have very hard, sharp beaks, which they normally use for breaking open mussels and crab shells. And it started biting.

And Gary started screaming.

Another thing about octopuses is that their tentacles are strong enough to capture sharks and break through the Plexiglas of aquariums, plus it outnumbered him by eight arms to two, and so it proved next to impossible for him to disengage the writhing creature. Yelling and tearing at the monstrous mollusc which was masticating his manhood, Gary staggered out of his bathroom towards the kitchen, looking for a weapon – a knife, maybe, to cut the thing off him, but even through the agony and the horror of what was happening to him he realised that this probably wasn't a good idea.

I may have mentioned that Gary's apartment had a balcony overlooking the canal, where he and his friends had been drinking earlier that evening. Fortunately it was one of those very muggy summer nights and he'd left the sliding glass patio door open, through which he could see the balcony table still littered with beer bottles. He knew he could use one of those to club the bastard thing off him.

He lurched onto the balcony and grabbed for one of the bottles just as the octopus gave a particularly nasty nip; he howled, jack-knifed in pain, overbalanced, struck the balcony rail, and pin-wheeled over and into the water thirty feet below.

Gary's floating corpse was discovered the following morning. The cause of death was recorded as accidental drowning brought about by alcohol, and although there was no sign of the octopus, his entire body was covered in numerous small triangular bite wounds which were officially attributed to rats.

As I said, this is a true story. It was told to me by a friend of the guy that died. But whether or not you believe me, one thing remains true. There is a delicacy which you can find in many of the canal-side cafes and restaurants in Birmingham and the Black Country – you'll have to ask for it specially because you won't find it listed on any menu – but if you're ever up that way I hope you'll try the local deep fried canalamari.

DIYary of the Dead

George Dewey stepped back from the wall in the upstairs hallway to assess his handiwork. The new wallpaper hung straight and clean, with the floral pattern matching exactly along each edge. Louise had made it clear how much she hated the design, but that hardly mattered now. She wasn't currently in a position to either hate or love anything. He squinted at it from several angles, looking for tell-tale shadows where the light caught...

Ah. There. Low down, just above the skirting board and approximately the size of a fifty pence piece.

A bubble.

Sometimes, with the best will in the world and no matter how methodical one was – and George prided himself on being a particularly methodical man – tiny air bubbles will collect under a sheet of freshly hung wallpaper and collect as blisters like this. It didn't bother him over-much; he knew how to deal with it.

Taking a damp sponge, he firmly but carefully smoothed it out, working towards the edge of the sheet, leaving it nice and flat again.

Then, with a tiny, almost inaudible little *fup!* sound, it reappeared. It was closer to the near-invisible line where this sheet joined its neighbour, and slightly smaller, but definitely there.

He pushed his glasses higher on his nose and frowned at the offending blister.

This should not have happened. The paper was heavy gauge, cloth-backed vinyl, the most expensive that B&Q could offer. He was an experienced paper-hanger; he'd redecorated their – sorry, *his*, he reminded himself – house every five years from top to bottom. This shouldn't have happened.

He took the sponge and smoothed it out again.

There was a little *fup!* as the blister popped up again.

This time it was on the other side of the join, which was physically impossible. The air in the bubble should have escaped when it reached the edge, but there it was. Staring at him.

Clearly this was going to take something a bit more drastic. He rummaged in his tool box for a Stanley knife, and frowned again when he couldn't find it. This too was most unusual – he was always so meticulous about looking after his tools. It was one of the many things which Louise, apparently, hadn't been able to stand about him. Well, that had gone both ways, hadn't it? He'd always hated her untidiness, though he'd never been such a nag as to keep on at her about it. Take the way her feet were sticking out of the bedroom doorway down the hall now, one shoe hanging off. Typical.

Then he remembered where the Stanley knife was. He went into the bedroom and saw it lying next to her.

'There you are, you little so and so,' he chided.

He took it through to the en-suite – added when the boys had grown too big for all of them to share the family bathroom comfortably – and carefully washed off all the blood. It was important to keep one's tools in good condition, after all.

'Meticulous,' he said to her as he passed back through the bedroom. 'From the Latin "metus", meaning "fear". That's what we call ironic, my darling.'

Going back to the impossible blister, he cut a single line precisely down its centre and smoothed each half down while the glue was still tacky. It would leave a barely perceptible scar in the paper when it dried, which was a shame, but he supposed that occasionally sacrifices like that needed to be made.

Louise had never understood the kinds of sacrifices which were necessary to have a well-kept and organised family home – not until the end, anyway.

He was going to have to do something about her clothes, which had sprayed all over the bedroom out of her suitcase when she'd swung it at his head. He didn't have a clue how to fold or where to put things like her bras, but he supposed he could just give them straight to a charity shop since she'd never be wearing them again. Especially the fancy frilly ones that he'd found she'd been buying secretly from Ann Summers, and certainly not wearing for his benefit.

There was a little *fup!* from low down, near the floor.

Directly below where he'd excised the bubble, another one of exactly the same shape and size had appeared in the paint of the skirting board. It might have been mistaken for a different one, but George knew better. And it wasn't just staring at him – it was openly mocking him. Just like she'd mocked him, with her fancy frilly lacy knickers and the other things she'd bought from that filthy shop. She'd waved one in his face and yelled 'Well why not? It's what I've learned from you, after all, isn't it? Do it your fucking self?' For a moment he wanted to smash and gouge that bubble from the wall with a hammer, a crowbar, his fingernails and teeth...

He drew a deep breath and forced himself to calm down. One thing at a time. Air blisters in paint required a different technique entirely.

He took the blister away with a paint scraper and sanded back the flaking edges with a sanding block, then primed the new bare patch of wood and went over that with some white gloss once it had dried. It took about two hours. At some point during the process he thought he heard a heavy slithering bump from the bedroom, but couldn't spare any attention from his focus on the job at hand. She'd always complained that he never paid her any attention when he was fixated on one of his 'bloody stupid projects', and he didn't see why that should change just because she was dead.

He made himself a cup of tea and went back upstairs to sit on their bed, surrounded by her lacy under-things and her blood which had jetted up the walls and swamped the carpet in a stinking red-brown flood. Suddenly his heart sank at the awful waste of it all. That carpet had been nearly fifteen quid a square metre; you didn't see that kind of value for money these days.

It vaguely crossed his mind to wonder where Louise had gone, but he had to finish his jobs first. One thing at a time.

As he reached the point where he'd repainted the skirting board, he heard a very familiar but much heavier *flump!* sound and the carpet beneath his bare foot lifted up in a blister as big as a cereal bowl. He actually saw it pop up, almost as if it had been trying to trip him.

'No,' he admonished it. 'Just...' He waved his mug at it for emphasis. 'No! Do you hear me?' Angrily, he stamped on the bubble.

The instant it deflated, his foot was seized by a savage cramp of agony, and a massive blister the size of a golf ball erupted in the skin on the back of it, close to where it joined his ankle. He yelled in fright and fell backwards into his arse. He grabbed his ankle, and without stopping to really think about what he was doing, pushed down on the blister with both thumbs.

It reappeared higher up, on the side of his calf.

He tried to massage it away, but it just slithered from under his grip and ended up behind his knee. Moaning in panic, he squeezed, kneaded, pummelled and punched his flesh to make the hideous thing gone, but each time he succeeded only in driving it higher and higher until somewhere towards his navel it disappeared. Instead of feeling victorious he knew with a sick certainty that this only meant that it was now inside him, and that his every movement – his every breath – was driving it deeper and deeper.

He froze, completely overwhelmed with terror and at a loss for what to do. This was the most terrifying thing of all: not what was happening to him, but that he, who was usually so capable, had no idea how to fix it himself.

And then Louise was there with the solution. Dear, sweet, loving Louise, who had forgiven him again as she had always forgiven his embarrassing, childish tantrums. She was finding it a little hard to walk, and he thought he must have cut some of the tendons in her legs accidentally, as she shuffle-slipped out of the family bathroom towards him, bumping against the wall and leaving a long smear of blood on his new wallpaper. One hand was demurely trying to hold together the slashed remains of her dress and her stomach, but the damage to her hands meant that they kept slipping open, revealing glimpses of her internal organs like an obscene burlesque act. There was no possibility that she might be alive, nor that she might talk – her throat was far too ruined for either.

All she could do was glare at him with the glittering intensity of her hatred as she handed him the thing in her other hand. The tool he need to finish the job. The Stanley knife. She wasn't going to spare the effort to kill him, and in the end she didn't even need to speak; the message in the offering was clear enough.

Do it yourself.

'I love you,' he whispered in a voice wet with tears of

gratitude and terror.

Slowly and clumsily, she finished her own job, which was to leave him.

The blister was still inside him somewhere, so he pressed the blade to his flesh and began to look for it.

The Curzon Street Horror

The carpenter who nailed down the final floorboard hammered as loudly as possible in a vain attempt to drown out the miaows issuing from beneath. When he was done he collected his tools and turned to the circle of darkly-suited men watching.

'It's done,' he said gruffly. There were tears on his cheeks, for, despite the roughness of his trade, he was a man with a love for all of God's creatures.

The man in the darkest suit merely held out a wallet, heavy with coin. Almost reluctantly, the carpenter accepted it.

Then he offered it back. 'I beg you, sirs,' he sniffed. 'Let me…'

The darkest man's gloved hand closed with firm authority around the carpenter's fistful of money.

'Do not embarrass yourself any more than you have already,' he said. 'And do not speak of this.' His hand tightened. 'Ever.'

The carpenter pulled away and fled, muttering, 'Monsters! Monsters, the lot of you!' while the cat's howls of agreement pursued him out into the midnight darkness of Curzon Street.

He glanced back and shuddered. In daylight he, like

many of the others who had worked on its construction, had been impressed by the grandeur of the new Birmingham Station, with its four monumental granite columns giving it the impression of an ancient Greek temple; it had seemed a fitting gateway to welcome the brave new Age of Steam. Now, in the suffocating darkness of a midsummer night, it resembled nothing less than a giant mausoleum, rearing over the souls who passed the dread shadow of its threshold.

'Monsters, he calls us,' mused the Chairman of the London-Birmingham Railway, as he locked the tall double doors. 'Alas, progress is ever seen thus. Gentlemen, let us prepare.'

The LBR Committee replaced their suits with long robes, and from boxes hidden in the customs cellar carried up items necessary for the ceremony: candles, a crate of Egyptian sand for marking out certain occult symbols, a translation of the ritual found inscribed on the walls of the great Temple of Bubastis, and a golden sistrum – a lyre-like instrument which the Chairman held in one hand as he consulted his pocket watch with the other. Finally, a box of mewling kittens was brought out. From within her place of entrapment, their mother, hearing the piteous noises, went into a frenzy of yowling and scratching.

Preparations made, the Chairman watched the second hand tick. At that precise moment, at the almost identical terminus building of the newly-constructed Euston station one hundred and seventeen miles away, an identical ritual was being readied with the other half of the litter and the kittens' father, who was similarly entombed. To create the mystical correspondences necessary to make the ritual a success, timing was imperative.

He looked up.

'Gentlemen,' he said, 'let us begin.'

*

The carpenter's name was Samuel Mills, and he went straight to the Fox and Grapes on Park Road – a favourite haunt of navvies, railway yard workers and canal-boatmen – resolved that if he could not refuse the money then he could at least use a good portion of it to blot out the memory of how it had been earned.

Unfortunately for Mills, he was of that breed of drinkers who become garrulous long before insensible. More unfortunately, he picked a public house frequented by railyard watchmen employed by LBR, who were fiercely loyal to their paymasters and did not take at all well to hearing them described as devil-worshippers and petitioners of infernal powers.

Four of them followed Mills as he left the tavern to begin his intoxicated meanderings homeward, and caught up with him in a secluded spot by the Fazeley canal, where they proceeded to deliver a savage beating – the intention being to warn him off future slanderous accusations. The third and most decidedly unfortunate part of Mills' evening lay in the drunken exuberance with which they set about him, such that by the time they stepped back to examine their handiwork, Mills lay senseless with his face an unrecognisable and bloody mess.

Fearful of discovery, his assailants threw him into the canal to drown, and melted into the night.

*

Five weeks later, on a warm July night, the Committee reconvened at Birmingham Station to test the success of their undertaking.

This time they did not enter the building, instead assembling by its main entrance. A young cat, one of the litter belonging to the dead and now thoroughly mummified adult, was brought forth. About its neck was a collar, attached to which was a metal tube capped in gold at both ends. One end carried the coat of arms of the London-and-Birmingham Railway Company while the other was inscribed with hieroglyphs indicating the name of the goddess Bastet: protector, mother, guide. Inside the tube was a message, the details of which were known only to the Chairman and his counterpart, who was currently waiting by the main doors of the corresponding Euston Arch terminus.

The cat rubbed about his legs, purring, as he took from his pocket a key whose design was a miniature of the sistrum which he had used to invoke the goddess' favour at their first meeting. It fitted the main keyhole perfectly, but had been created to open a very different kind of door.

Heavy tumblers rolled inside the mechanism.

He opened the door on a strip of absolute blackness wide enough only for a cat to slip through. A sudden draught issued from within; it was freezing cold and sharp with the dry perfume of ages-old incense and dust.

More than one member of the Committee took an involuntary step backward.

The cat inspected the gap for long moments in that particularly infuriating way felines have of remaining indecisive by doors, and then, with its tail high and proud, it stepped inside.

No sound or other disturbance issued from the blackness while they waited, until a faint miaow was heard from inside, and then out came trotting a similar, but obviously different cat – a brother or sister from the original litter. It too wore a collar with a gold-capped tube around its neck.

The Chairman bent to remove the tube, unrolled its contents and read them, and finally compared the message with one which had been couriered securely and secretly to him from his London counterpart several days earlier. With delight, he passed both to his colleagues.

'The procedure is a success!' he declared. 'We have proven the viability of instantaneous transit between two remote but correspondent locations. Gentlemen, this is an historical occasion.'

There was much fussing of the animal which had travelled so many miles in so few seconds and excited chatter and debate amongst the Committee members as talk turned to the future.

'The question remains,' said one sceptic, 'of how this can be developed on a mass commercial scale.'

The Chairman dismissed this with a contemptuous flourish of his golden key. 'When James Watt invented his steam engine, do you imagine he fretted over the details of creating a national railway system? No, that was for the men who came after him; he established the principle that *it could be done*. We still have years – decades, perhaps – of trial and experimentation ahead of us.'

'Can we be sure that it will even work with people at all?' asked another.

'Obviously, yes, as it stands the transit space is likely to be most hostile to anything other than our feline friends, and so the first thing we will need to do is modify the consanguinity vector of the ritual to incorporate human blood, but we have ample resources to work with there. Think of the surplus population of our city's underclass. How many disappear every day without being missed?'

'Like myself, do you mean?' growled a new voice.

It was Samuel Mills, the carpenter.

Miraculous though it was that he lived, nevertheless he presented a frightful apparition. His clothes were tattered, while his face was still swollen and bruised from his beating, and he pointed a heavy pistol at the members of the Committee with grim determination.

'You thought to have killed me, you bastards, but I've been watching you for weeks. Now it's your turn.'

'I'm sure I don't know who or what...' began the Chairman, and Mills shot him, quite simply and immediately. The pistol's report was shockingly loud. The Chairman fell against one of the columns, clutching his belly, his hand already a bright, glistening red. The rest of the Committee panicked and began to run.

'*Hold your ground every whoreson one of you,*' Mills bellowed. '*Or I'll shoot you down like the pack of dogs you are!*'

They froze.

Mills waved his gun at the station door, which was still ajar. 'Get inside. We'll talk about this in there.' He knew that the sound of the gun would quickly draw the local constables and believed that he could remain safe from them in the large stone building, at least until he could convince someone to investigate the truth of what he had discovered.

'You don't understand...' gasped the Chairman. 'What's in there is...'

'*Now!*' roared Mills. He grabbed the wounded man and shoved him towards the portal.

Faced with the unknown ahead of them but certain death behind, the members of the Committee had no choice.

Their counterparts who were waiting by the huge bronze doors of Euston Arch for further messages from Birmingham shrank back in horror at the figures which shambled through without warning.

White-haired and naked, the travellers wept and shrieked with laughter as they clawed at their own eyes and dashed their heads against the stone pillars. One was already bleeding profusely from a severe injury to its abdomen, and they were all covered in innumerable claw and bite wounds, as if during their transit they had been savaged by wild animals.

In due course they were rounded up and delivered to Bethlem Royal Hospital for the Insane, where, since it was impossible to verify any of their identities, they lived out the rest of their mercifully short existences in anonymous and irretrievable madness.

*

The whole affair proved so disagreeable to those who witnessed it that the Bastet Project was quickly and quietly buried, and LBR got on with the more mundane but comparatively harmless business of rail travel. Euston Arch was subsequently demolished in 1961 despite strong objections going as far as Prime Minister Harold Macmillan. One campaigner later wrote: 'Macmillan listened, or I suppose he listened. He sat without moving with his eyes apparently closed. He asked no questions; in fact he said nothing except that he would consider the matter.' Nobody knew that during that conversation Macmillan's fingers were toying restlessly under the desk with a small metal tube capped with gold.

Twenty years later, a mummified cat was found by construction workers under the floor of what was by then called Curzon Street Station. Rumours that one of the carpenters had also discovered alongside it a small golden key and kept this for himself have never been substantiated.

The Remover of Obstacles

The garage where Terry Grainger's car was getting its MOT was a quarter of a mile from the station, and by the time he'd slogged it there on foot, a grey evening had fallen. It had been a long day and he was sweaty, tired, and irritable. This place had been recommended to him as being only five minutes away – and he was left with a long enough walk to reflect fully on the irony that, of course, this meant five minutes by car.

His mood was not improved when he saw, in the parking bays labelled 'For Collection' an absence of anything resembling his car.

This was not to say that the walk itself hadn't been enjoyable, in a weird sort of way. Terry quite liked industrial estates. There was something stripped back, bare and honest about these places – as if you were seeing the city's true body, past the plucked and waxed flesh of suburbia to the oil-streaked skeleton beneath. True, it had been a relief to stretch his legs after enduring a day cramped in his office hutch, but he'd had to speed-walk in the midwinter chill to get here before they closed, getting hot and sticky in his thick coat, and all to find that his sodding car wasn't even ready. Terry hurried to the garage office, muttering darkly to himself and hoping that someone was still there who he could tear a few strips off.

The girl behind the desk looked through the sheaf of forms in his file. She frowned, puzzled, and then smiled up at him. 'You're in luck, Mr Grainger,' she said.

'Could've fooled me,' he scowled.

'There have been one or two niggles but it looks like your inspection has been Priority Fast-Tracked, which means you'll definitely get your car back by the end of the day.'

'Well that's something, I suppose, but how am I meant to get home now?'

He sighed, looked around at the garage office with its plastic school chairs and posters of dancing spark plugs. A paraffin heater was blasting out enough heat to boil water within several yards, yet the office remained chilly beyond that. With a half-smile of hopelessness he added 'I don't suppose any chance I can talk to Nick about these "niggles", whatever they are?'

'Certainly, sir. I'll just call him through from the workshop.'

Terry was taken aback. 'Really? Just like that?'

'Absolutely, sir. Just wait one moment.'

As owner and head mechanic of Nick Crewe Motors, the man himself had always been too busy, or unavailable, or on a call, or something else which prevented him from dealing with anybody so insignificant as an actual paying customer. To be granted access so suddenly and easily was like discovering that for years you'd been living next-door to the Pope without noticing. Plus, she'd called him 'sir'. Twice.

Priority Fast-Tracked, was he? Good; finally something was going his way.

Crewe was a surprisingly small man – though Terry thought maybe that was an advantage if your job involved crawling around under vehicles all day – dressed in blue overalls and drying his hands on a paper towel. He took the inspection paperwork and sat down with Terry to talk him through it.

'You got a couple of problems here, but the good thing is none of them's serious. One of the cylinders was misfiring, just a wiring issue, and we got that sorted out fine. The other thing...' he sucked air between his teeth and grimaced apologetically.

'Serious?'

'Not as such. Tricky, though. It's the exhaust: you got high carbon monoxide levels. Fixable, but a couple of the lads are off and I've got a backlog won't clear much before Monday. So what I've done is, I've run your car over to a mate of mine – exhaust specialist, he is – and he promises to have it done by tonight.'

'That's all very well, but I'm still stuck here, aren't I?' He knew he sounded peevish and ungrateful, but for heaven's sake, they'd had the thing all bloody day.

Crewe grinned obsequiously. 'Don't worry, it's not far. You can catch a number oh-nine-two at the bottom of the hill. Okay, so what you do is, you take this –' he pointed at where the bottom of the inspection form had been stamped with a red star like a primary school reward sticker for having behaved like a good boy. 'And you show it to whoever – bus driver, taxi driver, doesn't matter – and they'll get you to your car free of charge.'

'What – absolutely free? No fare?'

'Ministry of Transport, mate. We all work for the same people.'

'So what's to stop me just keeping this and using it whenever I like, forever?' he joked. 'Why do I even need a car, now?'

'It's only valid until midnight tonight,' Crewe said with surprising intensity, pointing out the small print. He didn't appear to find the situation funny.

'Sort of like Cinderella, then.'

Crewe looked at him with dark eyes in an oil-streaked face. 'No, sir. Not really.'

The bus from the bottom of the hill was crammed with so many rush-hour commuters that at first Terry thought he wasn't going to be able to get on. He showed the red star to the driver in his thick, assault-proof booth, who nodded Terry on without a word.

Though the journey wasn't long, it took him to a part of town he was unfamiliar with, a place of motorway flyovers, boarded-up pubs and scrap-metal yards. Every so often he caught the driver glancing at him in the big convex mirror that allowed him to see down the interior of the bus. Once, when Terry caught one of those furtive peeks, the man glanced quickly back at the road again as if having been caught committing a crime. It made Terry feel uncomfortably like an exhibit of some kind.

It also became obvious that there was something wrong with the route which the bus was taking. Nobody said anything aloud, of course, but it was there in the sighs, the snapping of newspapers and anxious glances out of the windows from his fellow passengers.

Just when he was beginning to get up the courage to ask exactly where it was they were going, the bus pulled to a sudden halt.

'Your stop,' the driver called back to him.

'Here?' He peered out of the nearest window, seeing nothing but factory units and lock-ups. A crisp packet and a plastic carrier-bag were duelling like drunks in the gutter. There didn't appear to be an actual bus-stop anywhere nearby. 'Are you sure?'

'Your stop.'

'Hang on a second,' objected a large woman with scraped-back hair and an obese toddler on her lap. 'Have you'm tekken us out of our way just for him?'

Disgruntled murmurs of agreement rose from her fellow passengers.

The driver flicked a switch, and the doors opened with a hiss of pneumatics. 'I think you'd better get off, sir,' he suggested, in the same sense that a lion tamer saying, 'I think you'd better get out of that cage, sir' was a suggestion.

He took it.

*

Where Nick Crewe had been small and dark, the proprietor of Imperial Exhausts was a wide, shambling sprawl of a man with a head so closely shaved and shiny that it looked like he was perpetually sweating. He pumped Terry's hand enthusiastically with a pair of big paws which had A-S-T-O-N tattooed on one and V-I-L-L-A on the other, as he apologised for the fact that the car wasn't actually in his workshop any more.

'So where is it, then?' Terry couldn't quite believe this was happening.

'Well you see, sir,' said the man cheerily, as he rummaged through a desk drawer, scattering stationery, 'the problem with your emissions was a doddle to fix. We got that sorted in about a half an hour. No, see, it was your brake fluid levels that was the problem.'

'Brake fluid.'

'Yes sir. Can't mess about with that sort of thing. Not enough brake fluid, your hydraulic pressure drops, and if you suddenly need to brake quickly – like, say a small child run out in front of you, well...' He stopped, gazing into the distance as if savouring the scene in his imagination. 'Make a hell of a mess, that would.'

'Um, yes, look...'

'It don't matter what anyone says – you can never get the smell out. Not really.'

Terry was acutely aware of how quiet the world outside this office was, as if the rest of the city had been deserted, and it was just him left alone with this man. This happy, possibly unhinged, absolutely huge skinhead...

'Here we are!' He slammed the drawer, having evidently found what he was looking for: a small stamp and inkpad. 'Can never bloody find anything around this place. Course, I en't used this in years.'

With great care and precision, he stamped another star next to the red one.

This one was green.

'There you go. All sorted. Priority Fast-Tracked. You take this and you...'

'Yes, thanks, I get the idea.'

The big exhaust man looked surprised, and a bit unhappy, as if he'd been interrupted in the act of delivering a speech he'd been rehearsing for ages. 'Right,' he sniffed. 'Well then. I suppose you know best. Let me just write down the address of the place where they're sorting your brakes. Specialist, he is.'

'Mate of yours?'

'Why yes, as it happens. D'you know him?'

'No,' Terry sighed heavily and rubbed his face with his hands. 'I don't know him.'

'Oh. Well, anyway, there's a bus stop just around the corner, get you there right as rain.'

*

As if to prove the point, it was raining when he got there.

PB Brakes and Hydraulics operated out of a row of semi-derelict industrial units backing onto the Birmingham and Fazeley Canal. Terry's nose detected it before his eyes did: the thick brown smell of stagnant water and rotting vegetation. Between walls of crumbling brick and rusted ironwork, he caught glimpses of weed-tangled banks and a detritus of plastic and Styrofoam bobbing in greasy water. Rain pockmarked the surface like acne scars.

There was no sign of his car anywhere.

In the workshop doorway gangled a tall, ginger-haired mechanic wearing the ubiquitous blue overalls, watching the rain and smoking a fag. Its red ember glowed in the gloom. He had an enormous nose which he kept blowing with great frequency and volume into a handkerchief so crusted with filth that it looked to Terry like it probably gave worse than it got, and his eyes narrowed with suspicion as he saw Terry approach.

'We're closed,' he said curtly.

'Um,' replied Terry, unfolding the wad of paperwork from an inside pocket. 'I think you've got my car in for some work on its brakes?'

The mechanic peered at the form. 'Don't know nothing about that. Come back tomorrow.'

'It's been Priority Fast-Tracked. Apparently.'

He sighed, and stubbed out the fag. 'Give it here then, Sonny Jim. Let's have a butchers.'

He took the paperwork and made a show of inspecting it closely, before taking out his mobile and dialling. He wandered away into the darkened workshop as he talked, and Terry edged in cautiously out of the rain.

'Hello, Steve? Phil. Yeah, no it's pissing down. Look, do you know anything about a blue Ford Focus with buggered brakes? Oh-nine registration. Got the fella here.'

He glanced sidelong at Terry. 'Fast-Tracked, apparently.' He listened. 'Yeah, definitely the type,' and he laughed wetly. 'Okay, cheers mate. Owe you one.' He folded up his phone, stashed it away, and blew his nose again.

'Wait here,' he said to Terry, and disappeared into the shadows.

Terry waited, standing in a small puddle of his own making.

When Phil returned he handed the paperwork back to Terry without a word. A blue star had been added to his collection.

'So,' Terry ventured, 'my car?'

'Oh it's not here,' said the mechanic, in tones which made it clear that Terry was only a step or two above being a moron for having suggested it. 'We sorted your brakes; there was a pinhole leak in one of the lines. Not serious at the moment but would have been very soon – good job we caught it when we did. Thing is, when we were under there we noticed some bad rust on the front suspension arms so we had to send it off to get that seen to.'

Terry was aghast. 'You what? This is ridiculous! I only brought it in for its bloody MOT! Is this some kind of idiotic practical joke?'

The mechanic sniffed. 'Had to, mate. Terms and Conditions. Nothing I can do about it. You don't mess with the Ministry.'

Terry more or less flipped at that point. His opinions on the Ministry of Transport in general and car mechanics in particular were broadcast loudly across the canal, including for good measure some observations on the weather, public transport, and little coloured stars. If it hadn't been for the shouting and swearing he might have been dancing, an interpretive piece based on the theme of 'impotent rage', which made up for in passion what it lacked in technique.

'That was interesting,' the mechanic said when he'd finished. 'Do you want to know where your car is or not? It's only just around the corner.'

'I give up,' Terry replied, panting and a little light-headed. 'Tell me.'

The mechanic told him.

'You have got to be fucking joking,' he said.

*

Redditch. They'd sent his car to Redditch.

He didn't even know where that was. The name of the place sounded like a frog farting.

'Just around the corner' turned out to be a Metro shuttle to New Street and then a half-hour wait for the connection, and as the train clattered up to the platform he saw with a sinking feeling exactly how crowded it was. He squared himself up to the familiar ordeal of having to force his way aboard, when a sour-faced ticket inspector plucked at his elbow and asked if he was the Priority Fast-Track customer.

'I think I probably am,' he replied.

'Very good. Your papers?'

He presented them for inspection, but the ticket

inspector wouldn't touch them; simply glanced at the star-stamps and flicked through the pages with the tip of his biro like a pathologist examining something particularly gruesome.

Terry had never travelled first-class in his life, and didn't believe that it existed on short-haul commuter services – which was why he was quite surprised to be led to the front of the train and into a spotlessly luxurious and completely empty carriage. His deeper instincts might have warned him that this was a little too good to be true, but they were drowned out by the complaints of his knees and his stomach, which had gone without much rest or food for nearly three hours. He sank into a wide chair and reclined gratefully. He thought he might have been offered something to eat, but the attendant disappeared almost immediately, as if he couldn't wait to get as far away as possible.

Then the train set off, and darkness slipped past the windows like an oil slick.

Once – just once – it seemed to him that something was keeping pace with the train on the other side of the glass. Something too big to be an animal, but too fluid of movement to be a machine. He pulled the window blind down with a shudder and dismissed it as the product of his overtired brain.

*

Redditch was the end of the line – literally so, because there were no through services. It was one of those large Midlands market towns which aspired to inner city deprivation but couldn't quite pull it off, its one notable feature being a massive cloverleaf junction joining two minor dual-carriageways, built with the grim optimism that one day there would be enough traffic to need managing – like a healthy man having double-bypass heart surgery just in case.

At least, that was the impression Terry got as Rajbinder the taxi driver swept him along its wide, empty curves on his way to Avon MotorCanics, which was allegedly where he would find his car at last.

Rajbinder disturbed him more than anybody else he'd met so far.

Despite being an obviously well-fed young man with a beard in which you could lose not just a badger, but most of the cast of *Wind in the Willows*, he was shy to the point of reverence. He seemed to be simultaneously terrified and elated at having Terry in his cab. He asked to have his photograph taken with Terry holding up his Priority Fast Track paperwork, saying that his wife would never believe him otherwise. Whatever that meant.

He also wanted to know if Terry would like to stroke the little elephant-headed statue on the dashboard for luck, but when Terry said that he wasn't sure whether he was currently in need of luck or suffering from too much of it, Rajbinder laughed nervously and said no, no, no, the luck was for himself.

'Why?' asked Terry. 'Who is this a statue of, anyway?'

'That's Ganesha,' Rajbinder answered. 'One of our most important gods – his name means the Remover of

Obstacles. It might be that he is like Saint Christopher to you.'

'Is that why he's got four arms?' Terry wasn't a Catholic; as far as he was concerned the closest thing to a patron saint of travellers was Jeremy Clarkson, and that was depressing enough. 'Is he like a cosmic traffic policeman or something?'

Another nervous little laugh. 'No, not at all. In his hands Ganesha holds each of the four elements: fire, air, water and earth. It puts him at the centre of the universe.'

Four elements. The centre of the universe. He couldn't quite put his finger on exactly what it was, but something about this rang a bell faintly inside Terry's mind – the sort of deep, slow bell one might hear at a funeral.

He passed the rest of the journey in an uneasy silence.

*

Avon MotorCanics was another anonymous industrial unit stuck way out in the middle of nowhere, almost in the Worcestershire countryside. If Redditch was the end of the line, then this estate was the buffer beyond which there was no track, and nowhere else to run.

Two cars were parked outside the garage – neither of them his. One was a large, sleek Beemer with its engine running and its brake-lights glowing like eyes. He asked Rajbinder to wait for him just in case, and knocked timidly on the door.

It was opened by an extremely large man dressed entirely in black – not large as in tall and gangly or fat and cheerful, but as in built of hard and highly-trained muscle. He had a bristling military-style haircut and an earpiece which trailed a length of coiled wire down into his collar. A second man, almost identical, stood further into the room behind a mechanic who was sitting at a desk, jigging one knee nervously.

Before Terry could even begin to form a reaction to this, the mechanic surged to his feet, exclaiming 'Finally! Thank Christ for that!' He tugged a cap down far over his eyes as if wanting to hide his identity, grabbed the paperwork out of Terry's hand, stamped it hurriedly without either reading it or making eye-contact, and fled, muttering something which sounded like, 'I want nothing to do with this. Nothing at all. You people are fucking insane.'

A motor revved into life and tyres squealed as he pulled away into the night at high speed.

Terry was left alone with the two black-clad men.

They looked at him.

'I don't suppose either of you know anything about rusted front suspension arms, by any chance?' he asked.

They slowly shook their heads.

Terry clutched his paperwork, which suddenly gave him a tremendous sense of security. The last star – which was some kind of orange-brown colour – had been stamped so hurriedly that it was little more than a smudge, like a smear of blood, or dirt.

Or Earth.

And suddenly, a lot of things fell into place in Terry Grainger's mind: the misfiring (fire) cylinder and the paraffin heater; exhaust emissions and the wind (air) playing with rubbish in the gutter; brake fluid leaking and the rain-swept canal (water); and now the earthen rust of his suspension and … what?

In his hands he holds the four elements. He is the Remover of Obstacles.

What went along with this, finally?

He didn't want to know. He really did not want to know.

'Right then!' he clapped his hands, hoping that he sounded cheerfully nonchalant. 'I'm good here, I think. I'm going to leave it for now – thanks all the same. I'll pop by tomorrow to pick it up. Or maybe next week. I can find my own way home.'

The man in black nearest the door was suddenly in front of it, blocking his exit, though Terry could not recall having seen him move.

'Don't worry, Mr Grainger,' said his companion. 'We're just here to escort you to your car, that's all.'

'That's very kind of you, but if you could tell me where it is, I can just…'

'It's parked in a secure location, sir. You can't "just", I'm afraid. It's all part of the Priority Fast Track service – can't have thieves and burglars interfering with your car now, can we? Not in this sort of area. It isn't safe.'

'Gypsies,' the man by the door added darkly. 'Place is crawling with 'em.'

'So if you'll—' The second man indicated the open doorway, which was now as miraculously clear as it had been blocked a moment ago.

They escorted him outside and into the purring Beemer. He noted with a dull lack of surprise that there was no sign of the taxi. It crossed his mind to make a break for it and run, but in all honesty he couldn't think of where he would run to. And besides, why should he? Nothing had been done to him – or even threatened. It had been a supremely strange evening, to be sure, but nobody had been overtly hostile or aggressive.

Nevertheless, it was strange to realise that as his rides had improved in quality – from foot to bus to first-class carriage to taxi and finally to the back of this luxurious motor – the places he had travelled through had become increasingly remote and desolate, and his sense of unease had slowly acquired the squirming weight of actual terror. But no, he couldn't run.

Then he was in the back, and both rear doors made quiet little chunking noises as they locked.

He should have run.

He lunged forward, gripping the shoulders of the seats in front of him, head straining between the two large men. 'What's going on?' he cried. 'For God's sake, where are you taking me?'

'We're taking you to your car,' repeated the second man, who was now driving. 'And also to see the Minister. He likes to deal with these things personally.'

The man in the passenger seat turned to Terry. 'I do hope you're not going to do something awkward, sir,' he said. Terry looked down, and from his angle could see into the front of the man's jacket, where something squat and gun-shaped nestled. He subsided. 'Mind you,' the man added, 'I wouldn't blame you. If I were you I'd be bricking myself.'

They drove him out into the countryside, along darkened roads so narrow that the bare trees arched overhead in a skeletal tunnel and overgrown hedgerows swiped both sides of the wide Beemer. He gradually became aware of a growing nimbus of orange light up ahead, and in gaps between the trees caught glimpses of motorway floodlights stretching away along a high embankment across the night-shrouded fields. By his reckoning it was the M40, which ran from the Midlands all the way to London. If he could somehow break free and make it up onto the hard shoulder, he might be able to flag down a rescuer.

The car stopped briefly at a chain-link gate which blocked the road. A sign on it read Motorway Construction: Authorised Access Only. The muscle in the passenger seat got out, unfastened a padlock, and they continued into a deserted construction site.

'As I said, sir,' said the driver. 'Quite a secure location.'

They followed a gravel service road past trenches and pits and great ziggurats of road-surfacing material, guarded by the slumbering forms of earth-moving equipment. Security floodlights cast long, sharp-edged shadows in all directions. Closer now, and above them, an unfinished slip-road curved up to the motorway, braced with scaffolding and half-poured concrete buttresses.

'Here we are.'

Finally, parked seemingly at random in the middle of all this, was his car. It was attended by a well-dressed man in a long coat and shoes which were much too shiny for a place like this.

'Mr Grainger?' He smiled, and shook Terry's hand.

'You must be the Minister.'

'Well, a Minister. Quite junior, really. So very good to see you at last. I understand you've had something of a busy evening. Do you mind if I just check that everything's in order?'

'God yes.' Terry handed over the paperwork with heartfelt relief. 'Just take it. All I want is my car.'

'Mm,' the other man replied distantly, reading. 'Yes, this is all fine.' He produced another reassuring smile. 'I know how you feel; I can't pretend that I enjoy coming out in weather like this, but still, we've all got our particular greasy pole to climb, haven't we?'

'Yes,' Terry agreed. The fellow seemed friendly enough. Maybe there was, after all, a perfectly reasonable explanation for everything. 'I suppose we've all got to make sacrifices.'

One of the guards made a choking noise, as if fighting back a sudden urge to laugh.

The Minister seemed taken aback. 'Well I must admit I am surprised to find you so, how shall we say, reasonable about the matter.'

Terry frowned. 'What matter would that be?'

It was then that he saw the long knife in the Minister's

hand.

And something huge moved in the shadows beneath the slip-road – something which might have had limbs like pistons, and a hide of scabrous bitumen. Something with breath that stank of diesel and the ages-old reek of human blood. It stared out at him with slitted headlight eyes, and he felt the heat of its naked hunger.

This time he ran.

He screamed for help until he was hoarse, until he found that he needed what little breath he could draw to keep running. Close behind, the guards pursued him with the easy, loping strides of men who were used to doing this sort of thing for hour on end with heavy packs across terrain much more demanding than this.

Heart pounding, lungs burning, legs quivering, he fled without thought into the surrounding maze of concrete and steel, taking turns at random, utterly lost, not even trying to find his way out because he had no idea where 'out' was, just heading as directly as he could to the bright lights of the motorway and the traffic where somebody – surely somebody – must see him. He fell several times, tearing the knees out of his trousers and the flesh from beneath, skinning his knuckles, and gasping as the liquid pain of a runner's stitch finally cramped him double.

Strong hands grasped him under the armpits and dragged him, struggling feebly, back to the Minister.

'…why…' he managed, as they held him, arms spread, face-down over the bonnet of his own car. Its otherwise sky blue colour was grey under the sodium light.

'Why?' echoed the Minister. 'Commerce and trade, man, why else? Because since the first motorway opened in 1958, over one thousand, six hundred miles of motorway have been built, and even though that is only one percent of the road length in the UK, it accounts for two thirds of all heavy freight traffic. You don't honestly think anything as valuable as that is going to be left in the hands of the engineers, do you? There are much older, much more tried and tested methods of keeping the country's lifeblood running.'

The bite of the knife across his throat was so swift and deep that for moment there was no pain at all, just a sudden, shocking torrent of blackness in front of him like an oil slick spreading across the car bonnet in which his face was reflected – eyes wide and white with terror. Then the pain struck and he realised that it was his own blood, black in the unnatural light, and he tried to scream.

*

They placed him in his vehicle with his hands on the steering wheel, his briefcase behind his head, and the spare wheel beneath his feet, and they arrayed about his body such talismans as would aid him in his journey: his bus ticket, his keys, and his shoes. Then they removed his car to a deep pit specially prepared at the heart of the new construction – the expanded junction of the M40 and M42 – and buried him beneath several dozen tons of hardcore rubble and cement, there to sleep forever, and keep the roads open.

The elements in his hands – the Remover of Obstacles.

When it was done, the Minister of State for Transport consulted his BlackBerry. He had an important ten o'clock which he couldn't afford to miss, but he had a feeling that the roads would be quite clear tonight.

Made from Locally Sourced Ingredients

Something flashed through the Land Rover's high beams and hit the front bumper with a heavy thump. Jeff let out a whoop.

'Got the bugger!'

In the passenger seat, Iain didn't reply. He simply reached into the back to gather his torch and a wide-bladed shovel as Jeff steered to a stop, killing the engine but leaving the lights on. They illuminated a stretch of hedgerow, and the empty lane ahead. Sudden and absolute silence enveloped them – the kind that only existed in unmarked country lanes at four in the morning. The engine ticked as it cooled.

'Felt like a big 'un, too!' added Jeff optimistically.

'Just get the cool-box, yeah?'

They climbed out. Jeff opened the back of the Land Rover and struggled with a large picnic cooler while Iain swept the ground with his torch back in the direction they'd come.

'See anything?'

Iain grunted a no. 'I think you might have only clipped it.'

'No way, man. I hit that fucker dead on.' Jeff dumped the cooler on the road and took his own torch around to the front to inspect the damage. Iain heard him muttering angrily.

'You know that big bunny catcher I had put on?'

Iain was only half listening, still unable to find their kill in the long roadside grass. 'Hm?'

'Yeah, well whatever it was, it weren't no fucking bunny. Look at what the bastard's done.'

Iain's torch stopped. 'Found it.'

He could only see one of its hind limbs poking out of the grass – the rest was an indistinct furry mass – but that was enough for him to tell that it was at least the size of a badger, if not bigger, and that it was still alive. The limb was twitching, long claws flexing against the asphalt as it tried to push itself to safety. Mercifully, it wasn't making any noise. He hated it when they squealed.

Jeff quit complaining about the condition of his ride and came back to see.

'How can it still be alive?' he wondered. 'How hard we hit it – no way. What the fuck is it, anyway?'

Iain stepped forward with the shovel raised, and aimed at where he thought the animal's head must be. 'Sorry about this, mate,' he said to it under his breath, and brought the shovel down hard. There was a flat, wet crunch and the twitching stopped.

'It's dead, is what it is,' he told Jeff. 'Let's get it on ice.'

They carried over the cooler, along with a second shovel, and between them managed to scrape and lift the carcass into it, chucking a couple of freezer blocks on top before clamping down the lid. Then they sparked up, leaning on their shovel handles and smoking into the night.

'Seriously, mate,' said Jeff after a while. His face was round and pale in the headlights, like an earthbound moon. 'I mean what the actual? It's not like any kind of badger I've ever seen. The teeth for one thing.'

Iain took a last drag on his cigarette and flicked the glowing butt into the darkness. 'You know, you think about this kind of thing too much,' he answered, and got back in the Land Rover. Jeff stood a moment longer, finishing his fag and staring at the long smear of blood which they'd left on the road, black in the red tail-lights. He shuddered, climbed back behind the wheel and drove them away.

After they were safely gone, something considerably larger than the thing stuffed in their cooler crept out of the hedgerow and carefully licked every trace of blood from the asphalt. It sniffed at the burning fag end, then at the trampled grass, and then finally at the smell of tire rubber which was still warm on the road.

Cautiously, it began to follow.

*

Alexander Rouse, proprietor and head chef of Savannah, the capital's premiere (and indeed only) freegan restaurant, narrowed his eyes in suspicion as Iain and Jeff opened the cooler. They glanced at each other nervously. They'd done unsavoury jobs for dangerous men before, and Rouse was right up there with the more barking of them. He was short and stocky, the story being that he'd once been a butcher, which accounted not just for the muscles acquired from a background of chopping carcasses apart, but also the particular speciality of his establishment. It took something of a psychopath to make a success out of even a normal restaurant, never mind one that used road kill in the cuisine.

'How fresh is it?' he asked.

'Don't you want to know what it is?' said Jeff.

Rouse turned the kind of gaze on him which gave the impression that he was assessing what kinds of joints could be cut from him.

'What are you, fucking David Attenborough? It's whatever I want to call it on the menu. The customers won't be able to tell the difference. All I need to know is how fresh it is so I don't poison any of them.'

'It's fine. Roaded it ourselves this morning,' said Iain, impatient for this to be done. The thing was giving him the creeps, even dead and lying in a box.

'Fair enough, then.' Rouse counted out their finders' fee from a fat roll of twenties. They dumped the carcass on one of his stainless steel work surfaces, pocketed the cash, and disappeared.

Rouse spent a while turning it to and fro, trying to get a sense of its anatomy, where the joints might be, the cutlets, the fillets – and more importantly, what the hell he was going to call it.

'You,' he decided, 'are a badger. You're going to be on

the *sett* menu, my friend.' Chuckling at his own joke, he picked up his skinning knife and went to work.

*

As the taxi pulled up outside Savannah, Lilla squeezed Patrick's hand in excitement.

'I can't believe you actually managed to get us a table here!' she beamed. 'The waiting list must have been horrendous.'

'Oh, not so much,' he shrugged. 'Only about six months or so.'

She laughed, then realised that he wasn't joking, and her hand went to her mouth in shock. 'My god, you're serious! But –' she did a quick bit of mental arithmetic '– we'd only been going out for a month by then.'

He smiled; perfect teeth in a clean-cut face. 'I like to plan ahead. Come on.' He got out, went around to her side and opened the door for her. Perfect manners to go with the teeth. She'd never have predicted that they would still be together after only a few dates, and wasn't sure how much life this particular fling had in it; to be honest, his forward planning scared her a little, but she supposed it was the sort of thing that made one a success in the City. Let him plan as far ahead as he liked. For the moment she was simply going to enjoy a night out on the arm of a handsome and embarrassingly wealthy young man at one of London's most exclusive restaurants.

At first sight, it wasn't all that impressive. It seemed to have been built out of distressed clapboard and reclaimed timber, with its name hammered together out of cut-up pieces of old road signs, like a ransom note. If not for the huge windows it would have looked like a farm shed dropped into the middle of the street.

Inside, once their reservations and coats had been checked, they found the same artfully contrived facsimile of urban decay. Bare walls, exposed I-beams, and no two tables or chairs alike. She loved it, and said so.

'*The Sunday Times* called it the Grand Temple of Freeganism,' said Patrick, holding out her chair. 'The philosophy of subverting modern consumerist culture by embracing found and foraged food. Or some such nonsense.'

'Which of course explains the outrageous prices,' she commented, picking up a menu. 'And the fact that you could buy several small African countries with the jewellery being worn in this place.'

'You,' he murmured, leaning forward, 'look completely gorgeous.'

'That,' she responded, 'was the correct response. You have been trained well, haven't you?'

'Not at all. This is natural, untutored smarm.'

She laughed. 'Oh shut up and tell me what I should be ordering. I can't make head or tail of this menu.'

'Funny, since that's probably what's on it.'

'Lovely.'

The menu, though short on courses, was long on information, providing explanations of how, why, where and when the ingredients of each dish had been sourced. The vegetables were grown organically in local allotments; the herbs foraged from patches of waste-ground; the trout caught from under the shadow of Big Ben despite the Thames having being declared biologically dead mere decades ago.

'And they really do serve up road-kill,' she read, shaking her head.

'Think about it, though,' said Patrick. 'Take a deer or a pheasant, say, that's been living wild. It's not going to have been force-fed all the chemicals and antibiotics that factory-produced cows and chickens have. It's going to be leaner and probably healthier, never mind that it died from a car instead of a bullet. Then there are the things you just don't get to taste normally. I think I'm going to go for the *blaireau au sang*.'

'What's that?'

'Badger casseroled in red wine with Armagnac and a glass of pig's blood. It's an old French peasant's dish, apparently.'

'Well your old French peasant can keep it,' she humphed. 'It sounds disgusting.'

'Possibly. But since it's also illegal to hunt badgers, one has to ask oneself: when am I ever going to get the chance again?'

'Let's just say it's not high on one's bucket list. I'll have the fish, thanks.'

Their food, when it arrived, was everything that the pretentious restaurant critics had praised. Their 'plates' were compressed discs of reindeer moss, eaten like poppadoms along with their main course, while their cutlery was made from peeled oak twigs carved at one end and raw at the other for them to chew as primitive toothbrushes. The starter – a terrine of venison, Trafalgar pigeon and foraged wild quince on a bed of toasted nettle and bittercress salad – was the roller coaster ride her taste buds had been promised, and her line-caught trout was meltingly wonderful, more inhaled than eaten. Patrick even managed to convince her to try a mouthful of his badger casserole. It was rich, heavily aromatic, and the meat was much less gamey or tough than she'd imagined for a wild animal.

'Interesting, isn't it?' he grinned.

'It's not what I was expecting at all.'

'Does it taste like chicken?'

'Why would it taste like chicken?'

'Surely you've heard that theory,' he said, surprised.

'What theory?'

'You know, that if you're eating something unusual for the first time it always seems to taste like chicken.'

'Is that the kind of thing you boys learn from watching Dave TV all the time?'

From a quick glance around, the *blaireau au sang* seemed to be quite popular with the other diners, and she found herself almost regretting her choice. But soon there was a new culinary adventure to distract her as the dessert arrived – praline shortbread wafers made with hazelnuts from the trees on Hampstead Heath, in an elderberry and rose-hip coulis – and its strangeness was pushed to the back of her mind.

*

Danny, the kitchen assistant (or galley slave, as liked to call himself, but never within earshot of that psycho Rouse), unhitched the locking bar on the big wheelie-bin in the back alley, flipped up the lid, and dumped in the sack of scraps which he'd collected. He did this automatically, without looking, and so didn't notice the thing whose head he dumped it on.

He heard it, though.

As he shut the lid, there came a tumbled sound of shredding and thrashing from inside, as if something large was tearing the bag apart to get to its contents.

Danny was no stranger to rats – nobody who worked in the restaurant trade in any city could be – but this sounded like a huge bugger. He couldn't work out how it had gotten in. Savannah, due to the kinds of ingredients it used, got more than the usual attention from Environmental Health, who had made Rouse get these special wheelie-bins with the lockable lids, and nothing that didn't have a thumb should have been able to open one. It could have been a junky, he supposed, but what kind of junky would be so desperate as to hide in a dumpster for scraps?

Either way, he didn't want to know. Hopefully whatever – or whoever – it was would eat their fill and sod off. Danny wasn't going to report it. It was the kind of thing that got places like Savannah closed, and Rouse was the kind of Chef who wouldn't just shoot the messenger – he'd skin him, wear his arse for a hat and eat his liver with some fava beans and a nice Chianti. In a pinch, Danny could always blame one of the Romanian cleaners.

The thing in the dumpster thrashed again, so hard that the bin actually rocked on its wheels.

Danny the galley slave shuddered and went back in to volunteer for washing-up duty.

*

Afterwards, Lilla and Patrick went for a walk by the river, finding a secluded spot where they could watch the city lights on the water twisting like broken neon eels. They were oddly beautiful.

'It's weird,' she said. 'To think that what I ate for dinner came from just over there this morning.'

'I think it's weird that you think that's weird,' he replied.

She frowned. 'Explain.'

'For thousands of years we – humans, that is – have eaten food that we've caught and grown ourselves. It's only in the last fifty or so that we've had this whole supermarket system going on. How sick must we be as a society that we can't see where our food comes from?'

'You say such sweet, romantic things,' she cooed, fluttering her eyelashes at him.

'I'm sorry, I'll try that again. That's a smashing blouse you're wearing, my dear.'

'Oh shut up,' she laughed, and swatted him.

And he disappeared.

That was her first impression, anyway; that her playful shove had somehow pushed him out of the world completely. The thing that came out of the bushes moved so silently and so fast that it bore him to the ground a dozen yards away before her brain had time to register the attack for what it was. Then there was just a tangle of flailing limbs in the darkness, Patrick screaming 'Get-itoffmejesusfuckingchrist GETITOFFMEEEE!' and the creature's own peculiar cry – a stuttering, indrawn mewling snarl. The thing (there was fur, she could see that much, and legs which seemed to bend in all the wrong directions as it scrabbled to maintain a grip on him), had its claws on his face, forcing his jaws apart, and its snout was right in his mouth, snuffling at him, *smelling* him from the inside out, while he bucked and yelled and she just stood there paralysed, watching, doing nothing. Why wasn't she *doing* anything?

Then it reached up with its hind-paws and tore his belly open, and she did something then. She screamed.

So did Patrick. Screamed and howled and begged and prayed and wept as it laid him open in the night air. Soon he stopped, but she carried on loud enough for the pair of them as she saw his intestines gleaming, just like the river had gleamed while they had been walking and talking a million years ago, and now she could smell them, the burnt-metal tang of his blood, the shit in his bowels, and – dear God as if that weren't enough – the meal he had lately eaten.

The creature dipped its head into the ruin and began to eat Patrick's dinner from out of his own dying stomach.

At this, her screaming turned to retching and she

stumbled away, bringing up her own meal as she went. It wasn't very far before all she could do was crawl, and the wet noises behind her continued as the creature finished with Patrick and moved on to what she'd left on the ground.

She didn't get very far. Its stink caught her first, making her whirl around out of some instinct to at least face the threat, just as its weight crashed into her, crushing the breath from her lungs. Its claws gripped her forehead and chin, forcing her mouth open, and its black eyes bored into her, obsidian and pitiless. She was nothing to it, she understood – just something to feed an appetite. Its muzzle pressed right between her teeth, slick with Patrick's death and its own drool, tusks against her lips, and she gagged, but her stomach had nothing left to give. The creature took several long, deep breaths of her.

Then it was gone, as quickly as it had appeared, and there was nothing but the broken serpents of light on the black river.

*

Through a fog of shock there were strobing emergency lights, faces, an ambulance, a hospital. People waved small torches in her eyes and asked her what her name was, did she know what had happened, was there anyone they could call – but they were on the other side of the fog and couldn't touch her. This was just as well, because there was something else on the other side of the fog which she didn't want to know about.

When it cleared a little, she found herself in a hospital

bed in a curtained-off resus room surrounded by strange machines and the bustling noise of an Accident and Emergency department.

The curtain was drawn back by a male nurse carrying a tray of swabs, dressings, and a bowl of water. Seeing that Lilla was aware of him, he produced a tired but warm smile. 'Hello, Miss. Back with us, are you?'

Words clambered over each other in Lilla's throat. 'I'm. In hospital,' she managed.

'That's right. Just a few scratches, that's all. There's a police officer outside who wants to ask some questions, but I told her she could just wait. We'll have you cleaned up right as rain soon enough. My name's Sam.'

Sam the nurse set the tray down on the bedside table and began cleaning her forehead. She sat patiently, like a child, and let it happen, watching the water become redder and redder. It reminded her of something on the other side of the fog.

'Patrick!' she said in sudden alarm. 'Oh my God! Patrick!' How could she have forgotten? 'Where is he? Is he alright?'

'The fellow who came in with you?'

She nodded. 'We were … we'd had a meal. We were going for a walk. By the river. Then a … a thing. It. Oh God…' she murmured woozily and flopped back against the pillow, fogged again. 'He's dead, isn't he?' she whispered, as if by doing so she could avoid drawing attention to it and thereby make it untrue.

The nurse gently placed a steri-strip across one of the

larger cuts on her forehead. 'Do you want to see him?' he asked.

No! thought Lilla. *Are you insane?* But nodded.

'Right, well let's get you cleaned up properly first. Do you have a name I can give?'

'Olivia,' she answered faintly. 'Olivia Martin.'

After some enquiries, Sam took her to a room and showed her a human shape under a sheet, but it wasn't Patrick. It couldn't be. It had his face and hair and the mole above his right eyebrow – it was in fact an excellent copy – but it simply couldn't be him. She knew he was dead, but that knowledge was out there beyond the fog, where it couldn't hurt her.

She was left alone for a moment, but Sam was back all too quickly.

'Miss Martin,' he said, still kind, but with a business-like edge to his voice. 'Sorry about this but we're going to be needing this room now. Can you give me a minute?'

'I'll, yes, I think so. What's happening?'

But Sam was bustling around the room, laying out trays of equipment and checking the machines while a porter came in and began to wheel away the bed in which not-Patrick lay.

'Where's he taking him?' she asked, startled.

'If you'll take a seat in reception I promise I'll get back to you about your man as soon as I can,' Sam assured her. 'Somebody's coming in hurt and they really need this room, sorry.'

Lilla backed gingerly out of the room, not wanting to

be in anybody's way, and as she did so she saw an emergency bed hurrying towards her, surrounded by a crowd of doctors and paramedics all talking medical gibberish to each other at the same time, and followed by a stricken-faced young man who was very smartly dressed except for the blood all over him. The patient was an older man entwined with tubes and wires, and his torso was heavily wadded with dressings which had already turned crimson.

Both men looked vaguely familiar – even despite the oxygen mask strapped over the face of one – and it took a moment for her to place them. The restaurant. They'd been several tables over; she remembered because Patrick had said he'd recognised the older fellow from a deal he'd worked on last year and wasn't it a small world? They'd laughed at the coincidence.

Lilla stepped aside as the bed rolled past, and knew that the huge, awful wound which lay beneath those dressings was no coincidence. She stopped the blood-covered partner as he staggered at the rear of the procession.

'It attacked you too, didn't it?' she said.

He turned wet, muddled eyes in her direction, but she doubted that he was seeing her very clearly. His mind was in the fog.

'It was so fast,' he replied vaguely. 'It didn't even look at me. Just went straight for Will.' Then his throat started working, and she knew that she had to be quick and cruel because he was on the verge of losing it altogether, just like she had.

'What did you have for dinner?' she demanded.

He frowned with confusion, and almost seeing her properly. 'What? Why?'

'At the restaurant. What did you *eat*?'

'I had the risotto. Will had the casserole. What does it matter?' He pushed past her and followed the paramedics.

Not a coincidence in the slightest. She felt herself becoming wobbly again, the fog pressing in on all sides, but shook it off angrily and went to look for that police officer.

*

Lilla found her seated in the waiting area, scribbling in a notebook.

'Excuse me, officer? You wanted to see me?'

The WPC looked up, taking in Lilla's haggard appearance – the blood, the taped-up wounds – then realised who she was and stood hurriedly.

'Yes! Yes I do! They told me you were being...'

Lilla cut her off. She couldn't be sidetracked. If she lost momentum the fog would get her again. 'Officer, my name is Olivia Martin. My boyfriend and I were attacked earlier tonight.'

'So I understand. Can you tell me exactly what happened?' Her pen was poised over the notebook, ready to record the nightmare in neat, safe handwriting. For some reason it made Lilla angry.

'That's not going to help,' she said. 'You need to get on

your radio and tell someone to go back to the restaurant where we had dinner, because I think other people are in danger of getting hurt.'

'I'm sorry, Miss Martin, I don't quite follow.'

'Those men who just came in,' Lilla pointed back along the corridor, 'were attacked by the same thing. Only it wasn't after us, not as such. It was after what we ate. That's why it didn't kill me – because I threw it back up.'

'Threw what back up?'

'The badger casserole.'

The WPC's mouth twitched at the corners, ever so slightly, and this just made Lilla's mood worse.

'I know how it sounds —' she began angrily.

'No, Miss, it's fine, honestly.' She plainly thought that Lilla wasn't playing with a full set of tiddlywinks. 'I'm sorry, I'm just trying to make sense of this.'

'Sense? *Sense*? Exactly what way of seeing my boyfriend get killed do you think would make sense to me, officer? You need to find everyone else who had that casserole and you need to do it now or more people are going to die!' She was shouting now, which was not wise. The officer stepped back apace sharply, the patronising smile switched off, and Lilla saw her hand move fractionally towards her belt, which carried such reassuring items as handcuffs, pepper spray, and a truncheon.

Lilla forced herself to calm down and backed away, hands in the air, placatory. 'I'm sorry. I'm sorry. Look, I just think I'll go and have a nice, quiet sit down. How about that?'

'I think that would be a very good idea,' said the WPC, still wary.

Lilla spent the next quarter of an hour doing anything but having a nice, quiet sit down. She knew that if she relaxed the fog would get her – or even worse, she'd have to think about that shape under the sheet. She knew that her parents were probably on their way, but all they would make her do was rest, calm down, and think. Every time the outer doors of the A&E department slid open she expected it to be another ambulance carrying a victim of the same thing that had attacked her. Could it really have targeted them because of what they had eaten? The idea seemed absurd. But if it were true, exactly what had they eaten to attract something that vicious?

Dear God, what had the chef at Savannah fed them?

*

The restaurant was dark and closed when the taxi dropped her off for the second time that night. She'd been in A&E longer than she'd thought; it was past midnight.

This was a mistake, she told herself. There was obviously nobody left. She cupped her hands against the window and peered inside: chairs stacked on tables and a closed sign hanging neatly in the door. No mangled corpses. No monsters.

Just a faint light far across the other side of the room, coming from the door to the kitchens.

The front door was locked, but with a little exploring she found a side alley which looked like it led to the delivery area. The problem was that there was no light down there; anything could be waiting for her. The only thing giving her enough courage to come this far had been her guess that the creature hadn't killed her before because she didn't have what it wanted, and the assumption that this still held true.

This was a *big* mistake. But she did it anyway.

The alley turned out to be harmless, and she came out into the yard behind the restaurant, cramped and stinking with boxes, bottles, and wheelie bins. The restaurant's back door was open, spilling light and the agonised moans of a man into the yard.

She crept closer to the sound, until she reached an angle where she could just about see into the kitchen. Saucepans and a shrapnel of broken plates littered the floor. She must have made some kind of noise without realising it, because a ragged voice called out.

'Hello? Is anybody there? Please, for God's sake, please help me!'

She edged further in, trying to see in every direction at once.

Alex Rouse, proprietor and head chef, was wedged in the corner of two cupboards, sitting in a spreading pool of his own blood. One hand clutched a carving knife, its blade black with the blood of the creature which had attacked him; the other hand was clutched to his stomach, and for a moment she wondered why he was holding links of sausages to himself. Then she realised, and shrank back against the door. He raised the hand with the knife, pleading.

'Hospital…' he gasped.

There was so much blood. She couldn't go near him.

'I lost my phone earlier tonight,' she apologised. 'Where's your landline?'

'Fuckin' hell,' he groaned. 'Mobile. In my coat. Back of the door.'

She found his coat on a hook and fumbled through the pockets for his phone, then, when he told her its PIN, fumbled at the phone itself, her fingers shaking with adrenalin. The first app she got was the last one he'd used: the photo album. She stared with increasing anger and disbelief at picture after picture of the road-kill that Rouse had butchered. Only by a massive stretch of the imagination could that thing be described as a badger. She waved the screen at him.

'What is this?' she demanded.

'What is *what*?' he retorted, and then screamed at the pain this caused him. 'My guts hanging out and you want to talk ingredients? Just call a fucking ambulance.'

'What did you give us?!'

He laughed, and screamed again. 'I gave you exactly what you paid for! Something gross to gossip about with your rich girly-girlfriends and your high-society arseholes. "Ooh, you'll never guess what I ate!" I could shit on a plate and you'd pay to eat it if some dickhead in a magazine told you it was trendy, as if any of you would have a fucking clue in the first place. I don't know what it is. I don't think anybody does. All I know is something else likes the taste of it a fucking lot, and if you don't call that ambulance soon we are both dead when it comes back.'

'What do you mean, *when it comes back?*'

He waggled the knife. 'I hurt it. I don't know how much. Maybe scared it off. Maybe not.'

She began to dial.

'Fucking finally,' he muttered, and his head fell back exhaustedly.

Something shifted in the darkened restaurant behind them. It sounded like chair legs scraping against the floor, as if a whole banqueting table of people had suddenly got to their feet at once.

'No...' Rouse moaned.

The connecting door to the restaurant slammed open and the thing which had attacked her leapt over the kitchen work top, scattering trays, dishes and utensils. It was like the thing in the photos only much, much bigger. At least the size of a wild boar – and there was something porcine about the tusks curving out of its muzzle, even though its body was long and low like a weasel. It stared at her for a moment, as if to confirm that she had no chance of stopping it, while Rouse screamed and tried to back away through the cupboards. Then it leapt down and buried its face in his midriff, finishing the job it had started on him as he kicked and shrieked.

Lilla ran – out of the kitchen, through the yard, along the alley and out into the street, completely forgetting about the phone and thinking only of flagging down a car for help.

The driver of the white van which hit her could hardly be blamed. He wasn't speeding, or talking on his phone, and did his best to miss her in a great panicked swerve, but still managed to clip the top of her right thigh with his front bumper and send her spinning like a dancer onto the pavement, where she struck her head and blacked out. What he did then was entirely blame-worthy, however. He stopped a hundred yards down the road and glanced in the rear-view mirror to see if there were any witnesses. The area was mainly industrial units, completely deserted at this time of night. He agonised for a moment. He already had six points on his licence and a thing like this would mean losing it for sure – along with his job, mortgage, house, and marriage, in that order. Hating himself, he made a quick, anonymous 999 call, and drove away.

*

The rannul limped out of the alleyway, after sniffing to make sure that it was safe. It had done its best to satisfy the primal instinct which told it to clear up after the remains of its dead pup, and the long night had left it near exhaustion. Across the road, in a patch of waste-ground between two warehouses, it smelled a gap in the world back to its nest in the Middens. But it had to be careful; the human female was lying over there.

It double-checked, and then ran across the empty road. When it was parallel with Lilla, lying half on the pavement and half in the weeds of the vacant lot, it stopped. Human was not the best meat – it usually reeked with pollution – but times were hard and it had been away from the nest for a long time. The rest of the rannul's pups would be hungry when it returned.

It took its road-kill by an ankle and dragged it away into the Middens.

The pups, it turned out, wouldn't touch the woman's flesh. They toyed with it and mewled and complained at its stink, until the rannul snarled its frustration at them and flung the human away, not wanting to kill it and pollute the nest with its blood.

*

When Lilla awoke, every part of her body hurt. Cautiously, she checked herself; scratches, bites and abrasions galore, but nothing serious other than a walloping great bruise on her hip which spread up her side and all the way down that leg.

It took some time for her to take in the details of where she was. When she did, she clamped her eyes shut and wrapped her arms around her knees, willing it to go away. This must be what insanity looked like. No sky should be that colour, the same bruise as her skin. No tree should move like that, clawing at the ground and screaming from a hundred tortured knot holes. Even so, she could still hear – the cries of animals which might have been birds, if there were such things as birds here.

She was in the land on the other side of the fog.

She wanted to be insane. She might wake up in a padded cell wearing a straitjacket and pumped full of anti-psychotic drugs, but at least this wouldn't have to be real.

But pray as she might, it didn't go away.

Eventually hunger drove her to her feet, flinching from the grass which writhed between her fingers. The message from her body was simple: eat or die. She'd survived being hit by a car and attacked by a creature from an alien reality, twice, and she was by no means ready to let something so pathetic as hunger kill her just yet.

Lilla tore strips from her clothing and bandaged up the worst of her wounds. She found a long stick which would serve as both a prop for her injured leg and maybe a spear, and collected enough small stones to fill her pockets, then set off to investigate those bird-like sounds and see if Patrick's theory was true.

She wondered how much of this new world tasted like chicken.

The Pigeon Bride

From the top of the Rotunda, a pigeon's beady three-hundred-and-forty degree vision takes in the Birmingham cityscape as a curved grey-green patchwork bristling with spires and aerials. Directly below, the Bull Ring development is a grinding chasm of concrete edged with the jutting ends of girders, as if the flesh of the city has been peeled back to allow something new – something clean and gleaming – to grow.

The pigeon took off, heading south over the site. The broad sweep of blue sky was an ocean above.

Lower.

The city tilted towards it, as mottled and multi-hued as its own wings.

Lower.

Rising from this, a tower. Smog-begrimed and scabrous with dereliction, nevertheless its windows reflected the late afternoon sun brilliantly, like a jewel trapped in the cage of its own setting.

Here.

Sarina looked up from her sewing as the flutter of wings at her window heralded his return. She tch-tch-tch-ed and left her work. Plenty of time for it later, alone in her room all evening. From her pocket she took some scraps of bread wrapped in a napkin, which she'd sneaked from the dinner table – Uncle did not approve of food in bedrooms – and crumbled them along the window ledge for him. Resting her chin on her crossed arms, she watched him feed, entirely unafraid of her.

'So, where have you been today, then, Prince Fisnik?' she murmured. 'Crap on anyone interesting?'

Fisnik fixed her momentarily with a beady eye, and continued to feed. She told him about her day – the unchanging injustices of school and home – mostly to practise her English but also because it was safer than writing anything down in a diary.

When he had finished, Fisnik regarded her once more with that same unblinking and business-like stare. She straightened up.

'Right then.'

Turning her back to the window, she pulled her T-shirt over her head and off. She tried to breathe steadily, tried not to let fear clench her muscles as she felt the needle-points of his claws sink into the soft flesh between her shoulders.

She very nearly succeeded this time.

*

Several hours later Uncle returned home and came straight up to inspect her work. By this time she had bound the wounds on her back and was sitting diligently at her sewing machine, its needle purring beneath her hands. She showed him how much of the material she had used, the quality of the pieces she had made so far, and suggested that her quota might even be completed early tonight. He grunted by way of response.

'If there is time…' she ventured.

'No,' he replied curtly, and then appeared to soften. 'It is not safe for you to go out after dark. The streets are full of dangerous people. I promised your father that I would look after you and that is exactly what I mean to do.' Yet there was a hardness hidden beneath the soft edges of his words which she heard well enough.

'But Uncle, I go to school all day and there is so much work to be done in the evening…'

'There is so much work to be done because your father's debt to me is so big. Surely you appreciate this. Your father was an honourable man and would have worked all his waking hours to repay me – surely you wish to honour his memory, don't you?'

It was an old argument to which, as ever, she had no reply.

He hesitated at the door. 'Sarina, there is something you should know. I have made an arrangement which will secure your future in this country and go a long way to clearing your debt. He is a handsome young man, very wealthy, also from Albania. He will be coming to dinner to meet you tomorrow night. Look to preparing something fit for the meal.' He left, locking the door behind him.

*

Nor was that the end of his demands. Towards midnight he came to her as usual, stinking of cigarettes and alcohol.

His weight pressed the wounds on her back deeper into the mattress and the pain burned like fury, but it allowed her to escape. She lost herself in memories of other pain – crossing the Adriatic with her father on a ship so crowded with refugees that sleeping on deck in the rain was preferable to the prison-hulk conditions below; hiding and running north for weeks through Italy and France, half-starved; months of tedium in the purgatory of Sangatte; and finally, crammed in the back of a container lorry paid for by the man who now claimed the title of Uncle for himself, discovering too late the lack of ventilation, face pressed by her father against the crack where floor met door, gasping at meagre sips of air as he choked and died, with not enough air in her lungs even to sob goodbye, falling into unconsciousness; falling back into herself…

…as he pulled away from her, zipping himself back up in the darkness. He stood awhile, a deeper blackness in the gloom, a black hole taken the form of a man. He'd never lingered like this before, and suddenly she was terrified of what this implied.

'This young man,' he said finally. 'He expects that you are to be a virgin.' No more than that, but his voice was lifeless, like a dead man's, and she knew with an insight as powerful as the terror which had caused it that if she stayed, she too would die.

*

Fisnik kept his appointment the next day, and as ever she fed him with what she'd been able to sneak from the table, and poured out her grief to him. 'So it has to be finished now! Somewhere else! Somewhere soon!' She wept. 'There's no time to do it safely, and it can't be done here. Uncle is watching everything I do; the moment he hears anything I'm finished. Do you understand?'

It appeared that he understood. He took wing, and she watched him dwindle to a speck in the sky over the city centre, and finally disappear. She waited for what seemed like an age, too nervous to contemplate any of her evening's piece-work, though in truth it could not have been longer than an hour. The tenacious light of a summer evening slipped towards dusk a feather's breadth at a time.

Eventually, a dull roar of wings announced his return, accompanied by hundreds of his companions. They crowded into her room, murmuring and milling around on her shelves, on the bed, dropping their little white turds all over the carpet and her sewing. Uncle would be furious, but that hardly mattered now.

'Right then.'

She stretched face-down on the bed, Fisnik's company moving respectfully aside for her, and at some unseen signal from their prince, they descended upon her in a cloak of wings.

*

Downstairs, it took a while for her Uncle to notice, above the television's burbling inanities, the noise of what sounded like a thunderstorm blowing directly into the flat. He snapped off the TV and glared at the wall where her room was. Now it reminded him of waves – huge wind-driven rollers dashing themselves against the walls of the girl's room, making the light fittings dance like hanged men. He hauled himself off the sofa and stomped into the hall shouting 'Sarina! What in Christ's name are you doing, girl?!'

He paused by her door. It was much louder out here. Nothing he could imagine her doing could account for such a noise, and he felt fear uncoil itself greasily in his gut. This in itself was enough to make him wrench the door open and stride in furiously.

His sight lasted barely longer than a few seconds after opening the door, but in that time he registered everything with hideous clarity.

Pigeons filled the room like a cyclone, and Sarina's body was a living carpet of wings. The birds had shredded her clothes instantly and kept going: hundreds of beaks glistening red as they rose and fell, rose and fell like the purr of a sewing machine needle transforming shapeless material into an elegant garment. They completed in minutes the task which would have taken Fisnik weeks alone – not out of malice or even hunger, but simple gratitude. Gratitude for food given despite her own hunger, for selflessness in the midst of her own misery, for protection, for love. Her back was a morass of blood, with her twin scapulae gleaming pink on either side of the corrugated ridge of her spine.

And then they had set her free.

A wing, as large as that of an albatross, yet roseate

with blood and crumpled as an emergent butterfly's, broke free from the body and rose above the sea of pigeons, flexing slowly.

The storm of wings rose from the bed and moved to the window, passing him as it did so, and a small number of pigeons broke from the main body long enough to fly at his face. Shrieking, he fell back, too late to protect his eyes from being gouged out of his head in globs of molten agony, and thus he missed her final transformation.

The dense cloud of excited, exultant birds dropped from the window thirteen floors up in the tower that had been her prison and dispersed, accompanied by something large and white and exquisitely graceful which soared up into the sunset clouds with them while the last remnants of her old flesh plummeted earthwards.

So enraptured was she in the joy of her new life, that she didn't even bother to mark where it fell.

Tourmaline

(Extract from the novel)

Taken from the Operations Handbook for DCS Field Agents (17th Revised Edition); Appendix D: Non-Suborned Threats. Reproduced by kind permission of the Department for Counter-Subornation.

...the araka is an extremely pernicious d-sentient parapsyte which sustains itself on the emotional trauma it causes by compelling its host to perpetrate acts of humiliation, degradation, and beastliness. Infestation is mercifully rare – confined predominantly to the lower-class slums of large conurbations and the ghettoes inhabited by foreigners of known moral dubiety – yet the danger an araka presents to the unwary agent cannot be underestimated.

In its natural state – if indeed it can be said to possess such a thing – the creature inhabits the lowest levels of its host's psyche, close to the threshold of the collective unconscious, which it uses to pass from host to host during sleep; the araka shuns the bright light of consciousness, preferring the crushing blackness of the chthonic depths. Whilst there can, of course, be no objectively verifiable information regarding its appearance, certain commonalities of description have been observed in the insane ramblings of those who claim to have seen one, to whit: writhing multitudes of tooth-lined tentacles proceeding from an integument of horned and overlapping plates. However, in the case of an infected host falling victim to a subornation Event, the araka invariably takes advantage of the Event's protean nature to detach from its host – assuming a form which even to the experienced eye is indistinguishable from the Event's other actants – and hunt for a new host.

Being non-human – and in any event only partially physical within the boundaries of the Event – the araka remains unaffected by the standard arsenal of sal volatile aerosols and tezlar guns. If the agent is fortunate, it may content itself simply with tearing him limb from limb and feasting on the fear -drenched tissues of his brain. If he is unfortunate, the araka may attempt to infiltrate his consciousness completely, turning him into a puppet of flesh for its hideous and abominable appetites.

Thus the advice given to any Counter-Subornation agent who believes he may be in the proximity of such an entity is simply this:

Run.

Chapter One

She Shall be Called Woman

1

Squalling rain chased the young woman up the steps of Birmingham University's Barber Institute of Fine Arts and into the shelter of its wide doorway, where she rested for a moment, shaking the water from her coat and combing back damp hair with her fingers.

Neil Caffrey, nearly at the end of his six-'til-three shift on the main security desk by the gift-shop, nudged his colleague Steve, who was frowning at the Guardian crossword.

'Oi-oi,' he murmured, 'bandits, two o'clock.'

Steve glanced up and then back down at his paper, shaking his head with a smile. 'Don't you ever think of anything else?'

'What's to think about?' grinned Caffrey. 'Man, she is fit.'

'She is a *student*, is what she is. Don't you like this job, or something? Quickest way to get sacked, mate.'

'Never happen. And even if it did, Christ, it'd be worth it. I want to die between those legs.'

'Yeah, well, you better be wearing flameproof underwear, because you are going to crash and burn, my friend. Crash and burn. Still, whatever,' and he waved Neil on with the end of his biro. 'It's your funeral.'

'Roger that.'

Caffrey put on his best professional security guard smile and sauntered over. The girl was not just fit, he decided – she was gorgeous. Her blonde hair had darkened with the rain, and as he got closer he saw that she had the most incredible sea-blue eyes. Hard to tell about her tits under the coat, but then he liked a bit of mystery.

'Can I help you, miss?' he asked, with just enough emphasis on the 'help'.

'Oh yes, please,' she replied, looking genuinely

relieved. 'I'm looking for a painting.'

'Well you've come to the right place!' he grinned. 'We've got all sorts. Finest collection of French Impressionists outside of the National Gallery and more Pre-Raphaelites than you can poke a stick at.'

'Well it's really only one painting in particular that I'm interested in. *She Shall be Called Woman*, by George Frederic Watts. I understand that it's on loan from the Tate. Could you please tell me how I can find it?'

'I can do you one better than that: I can take you to it myself.'

'Oh no, you really don't need to go to the trouble…'

'No trouble at all, Miss. This place is a bit of a maze.' The layout of the Barber was actually about as complicated as a Wendy House, but a few careful detours would give him plenty of time to work the old Caffrey magic.

'Well, I suppose, if you say so…'

Caffrey led her up the main staircase towards the first-floor galleries, pausing only to leer back over his shoulder at Steve, who mouthed the words *crash and burn* back at him.

2

It didn't take Caffrey long to realise that Steve had been right: he wasn't going to get anywhere with this girl.

He managed to get her name – Vanessa – and the fact that she wasn't a student but had travelled up from London, which didn't make any kind of sense, because why would you travel from London to see painting that was on loan from a London gallery? Beyond that her answers were monosyllabic and distracted; she kept twisting the strap of her handbag and running on ahead into the next room, despite his attempts to slow it down and draw her out with a bit of chat about some of the artworks which he knew the ladies always went for. Funny how they'd get all excited about a bronze statue of some wood-nymph with her tits out, but stick on a dirty DVD and they slapped you in the face and called you a pig. Just couldn't figure them.

And she was off again. By the time he caught up with her, she was around the corner and too far down the next corridor for him to stop her doing what she did next. The only other person in there besides themselves was an old man on a bench, and he looked like he was asleep, or possibly dead. It wouldn't have been the first time.

The painting that she was heading for was massive – had to be six foot high if it were an inch – and it showed a woman's upper body emerging from a swirling riot of leaves and birds. Flowers bloomed beneath her right hand and a mantle of golden cloud opened around her shoulders and down to her navel as if she was bursting free from some kind of cocoon. But she was cloudy and indistinct: her face thrown back and in shadow, her breasts mere suggestions. It was as if she were awakening fully formed into life without knowing who she was supposed to be.

The impression struck Caffrey so forcefully that at first

he didn't realise that the Vanessa woman had stepped over the low brass barrier rail and laid her hands flat smack on the painting. Her head was bowed, and her breath heaved as if she were suffering the world's worst asthma attack.

Caffrey snapped out of it.

'Hey! Er, excuse me, Miss? I'm afraid you can't actually…' He reached out to grasp her shoulder, and his voice died as he saw what was happening.

The paint beneath her hands was moving.

3

Steve McBride looked up in surprise as the rain-soaked woman ran back past the security desk. She glanced at him briefly – a wide-eyed, haunted expression – and was outside before he could open his mouth to ask if she were alright. Standing in the doorway, he watched her run down the campus drive towards where it joined the busy dual carriageway traffic of the Bristol Road, and then she disappeared.

Nice one, Neil, he thought. *A personal best. In what world does 'chat up' mean 'drive screaming from the building'?*

He went back to his crossword.

Ten minutes later, when Caffrey had failed to materialise, he chucked it down again and went to look for him.

Steve found his ID lanyard on the floor at the corner of the Blue Gallery (art 1800 to 1900), in front of the painting which the young woman had been asking after, and there was a strange smell in the air which he almost recognised, but no sign of the man himself. There was no sign of him anywhere in the entire building, come to that. He wasn't lurking outside, having a crafty fag. Steve ducked across the road briefly to the Guild of Students to see if he were taking an unofficial coffee break, mindful that if he was caught leaving the desk unattended it could cost him his job, but Caffrey wasn't there either. Nor was he answering his phone – not his mobile, not at his flat. At the end of his shift, Steve even went around to drop the lanyard off – although it had crossed his mind to keep it and let the silly sod take the consequences of an ear-bashing from Peterson, their supervisor, for losing his ID – but there appeared to be nobody in. Nobody answered the buzzing intercom, and no lights were on in the window. At which point Steve concluded *sod this,* and went home.

All of it completely drove from his head the trivial detail of the peculiar smell which he'd noticed in the Blue Gallery. It was only long afterwards – after he'd fallen in love with Vanessa Gail, and the horror which she had unleashed had gone too far to be stopped – that he thought back on it and realised what it was: the smell of the sea.

4

The wake which trailed after her through the Institute's doors and down Edgbaston Park Road was picked up by one of the Hegemony's floating sensor buoys, but even if she'd been aware that such things existed, she'd never have noticed it, since it looked just like any other homeless young man sitting blank-eyed and motionless, huddled at a bus-stop, easily ignored on a busy city street.

To the buoy, her wake was perceived as a fading, v-shaped distortion in the meniscus of reality, something like a ripple of heat haze. Beyond that, it was entirely unaware of her existence. In its natural state the creature was something like a large, semi-sentient jellyfish, which swarmed with millions of its kind in shallow tropical waters and grazed on the microscopic fragments of dreamwrack left by sleepers. The detector sense which allowed it to home in on their presence served the Hegemony's needs for a simple, passive early warning system, and they were common enough to be deployed in large numbers throughout most major cities, but it wasn't sophisticated enough to provide any details beyond a simple imperative: *prey here!*

It didn't follow her. That was not its function, since it lacked the necessary autonomy or imagination that might allow it to anticipate a human being's behaviour. However, there was just enough consciousness left in the vessel which carried it to perform basic, well-trained actions.

From within its filthy clothes, it produced a mobile phone and sent a single preset message to the only number the phone could reach.

The call's time and geographical location were logged automatically into a system which routinely received thousands of such calls a day, and it began a slow, upwardly-sifting journey through a series of filters and subroutines designed to trawl through the background chaos of the world and isolate preciously rare fragments of purpose. It was weeks, possibly even months, away from the point where a living, breathing operative might see it – if at all.

But that was the thing about hunting. Sometimes it required a level of patience that was almost inhuman.

5

Caffrey didn't show up the next day either. When Peterson called him into his office and asked if he knew anything about where Caffrey might have gone, Steve confessed his ignorance and produced the lanyard, earning a reprimand which he totted up on his mental account sheet of Shit That Neil Owed Him For. He wouldn't have gone so far as to say that Caffrey was one of his best mates, but they'd worked together often enough to have developed a rapport, which was close enough. Still, Steve had given him a chance; if Caffrey wanted to play silly buggers or had gotten himself into trouble then that was his own lookout. Equally, if Peterson wanted to call the police and report him as missing, then that was fine too. Steve had learned long ago that the security industry attracted a sizeable proportion of the kind of people whose murky pasts you did not want to get involved with, and if Caffrey turned out to be one of them, he was better off out of it.

It never crossed his mind that it had anything to do with the girl. Caffrey had tried it on with so many others and been shot down so many times that his skin was thicker than his head, and the idea he might have done a runner over her was just laughable.

Then, precisely a week later – and even at the same time of day – she was back. He could hardly miss her; the April weather had turned warm and sunny, and she walked past his desk wearing sunglasses and short blue dress which showed an awful lot of leg.

He followed her upstairs to the galleries, not at all sure of what he was going to say to her. He could hardly accuse her of having kidnapped Caffrey, and anyway there was something a bit off-putting about the relentless way she headed straight for the Blue Gallery. The Barber Institute was a work of art in itself: a Grade 2 listed piece of award-winning Deco architecture which boasted collections from Botticelli to Magritte and one of the biggest collections of ancient coins in the country, and she was walking right past everything (with those very shapely legs), as if none of it were there.

He caught up with her in front of *She Shall Be Called Woman*. She'd taken off her sunglasses and was gazing at the painting – rapt but serene. There was nothing of the haunted panic he'd seen last time. It was like looking at a different woman.

While he was still trying to work out how to approach this, she spared him a moment of her attention.

'Can I help you?' she asked.

'To tell you the truth, I'm not sure', he replied, and faltered. Indicating the painting, he said: 'If you don't mind me asking, what's the appeal?'

'Of this?' She shrugged. 'It's a personal favourite.' As answers went, it told him precisely nothing. 'Is that what you wanted to ask?' There was dry amusement in her voice.

'Well, no. See, the thing is…' he rubbed the back of his neck and looked away awkwardly. 'The last time you were here, you were escorted by my colleague.'

'Neil. He introduced himself.'

I'll just bet he did. 'Yes, well the problem is that since then he's sort of gone missing.'

'That was dramatic of him. No offence to your friend, but he didn't strike me as being that imaginative.'

'And I think you were the last person to see him, and I just wondered if he said anything to you which might shed some light.'

'Not really. Sorry.'

'He didn't – I don't know – *invite* you anywhere?'

'Invite me?' she laughed. He got the impression that she was laughing at the idea rather than him, and found that he liked the sound of her laugh very much. He wondered how a man went about making a woman like this laugh a lot more. Probably not by criticising her taste in art. *What's the appeal?* Jesus. He cringed inwardly. 'I'm sorry Mister,' she peered at his ID badge 'McBride…'

'Call me Steve.'

'…but your colleague didn't invite me anywhere. He

came on a bit strong and I said I wasn't interested – several times, in fact – and then he called me a frigid bitch.'

'Oh Christ, I'm sorry.'

She continued quite matter-of-factly: 'Not to my face, of course, but loud enough for me to hear it, so I threatened to complain to his supervisor – *your* supervisor, I suppose – and he stormed off. Look, don't worry about it.' She waved away his apologies. 'I've been called a lot worse. He'll be off nursing his bruised ego somewhere.'

Steve's relief was palpable – it felt like something unknotting itself below his ribs. He should have known it would be something that simple. All the same, if Caffrey had shown his face at that precise moment Steve would cheerfully have punched him in it.

'So anyway,' she added, 'I think I'm done here for the moment. It's been a pleasure to meet you, Mr McBride.'

'I said call me Steve.'

'And I said it's been a pleasure.' She held his gaze a little longer than was strictly necessary, and turned to go.

'Can I just say again how sorry I am for all of this?' he blurted.

'Please don't. It's starting to sound a little creepy now, and you made such a good first impression.' Leaving him utterly tongue-tied, those incredible legs carried her out of the building.

It was only after she'd left that he realised he hadn't even got her name.

6

That evening he presented the conversation to his kid sister Jackie for inspection. She was getting ready for her fortnightly Girls' Night Out while he took care of dinner time for her two boys, Mark and Will. Uncle Steve's culinary skills didn't run to much more than fish-fingers, chips and peas, but that was fine with them, being only six and eight years old respectively. They threw food at each other in front of Nickelodeon while he scrubbed vainly at the scorched mess that he'd made of the grill pan, and Jackie drifted in and out of the kitchen, demanding forensic detail of the encounter.

She stopped, fiddling with an earring. 'She said what?'

'That it had been a pleasure,' he repeated.

'And then she looked at you?'

'Yep.'

'How did she look at you?'

'What do you mean, how did she look at me?'

'Well, was it a look or a Look?'

He thought about it. 'I don't know. Maybe it was a Look.'

'And then you said what?'

'Well I didn't know what to say, did I?'

Jackie groaned in despair and whacked him over the head with a spatula. 'You great nurk, that was it! That was the come-on and you missed it!'

'How is a Look a come-on?'

'What did you expect her to do – wrap her legs around your waist and say "Take me now, Big Boy"?' He resumed scrubbing glumly, and she drifted out again but returned a few moments later, hopping on one foot while doing up a shoe – one of her self-confessed 'slut-pumps'. 'Next time she shows, you have to ask her out,' she decided.

'No, I've buggered it now, haven't I? A girl like that – she's never going to go out with a bloke like me.'

'Not if you keep coming out with self-pitying crap like that, she's not.'

'Thank you for your support. I shall wear it always.'

Jackie stopped wrestling with her shoe and seized him in a fierce hug from behind. 'Listen, big bruv,' she said. 'You are a six-foot-one security guard who looks a bit like Ben Affleck in a flattering light, likes kids and can sometimes hold a conversation which isn't about sport. Admittedly you can't cook to save your life, but that just proves you're not actually gay. There are thousands of women in this city who would throw themselves at a bloke like you, believe me. I can still set you up with one of the girls from work, if you like.'

'No bloody fear. I ended up needing stitches last time, remember?'

'Suit yourself.' She gave him a peck on the back of the head and breezed away in a cloud of *Ange Ou Demon*, singing La-Gaga's 'Born This Way' cheerfully off-key.

Later, when his nephews were tucked in, he fired up Jackie's laptop and googled She Shall Be Called Woman. It had been painted by George Frederick Watts, who was apparently considered to be one of the greatest Victorian artists, and was supposed to be the central of three paintings depicting the creation, temptation, and eventual repentance of Eve. Steve had no idea how this helped him at all, except that maybe it gave him something to talk about to the woman in the blue dress.

But over the next few weeks he was never able to quite bring it up.

She came by at precisely the same time each Friday, giving him a polite smile and a little nod of recognition as she passed his desk, went upstairs to commune with Eve, and then left. She never lingered to examine any other artworks, and she never stopped to chat, and each time that he failed to start up a conversation with her made it harder the next time. He may well have made a good first impression, but at the moment he was performing a painfully slow crash-and-burn all of his own. This, he was sure, would have continued until the painting returned to the Tate and she disappeared from his life forever, except that she crashed first.

Reprinted with permission.
First published by Snowbooks © 2013 James Brogden

Afterword

'The Phantom Limb': This was written as a winning entry for Den of Geek's short horror story competition *Den of Eek!*, a cancer charity fund-raising anthology <u>which you should buy</u>. It's based on the idea that amputees often experience phantom pains in their non-existent limbs, and expanded to imagine what would happen if such a person could start to feel things in that place where their ghost-limb is – and what if something on the Other Side shook hands.

'The Evoked': Aussie Christmases are weird. You either have them in the middle of summer or in July – whichever way you look at it, something's off-kilter. Hence this. I wrote it while on a training course about how to teach English for the International Baccalaureate – it seems to me that writing horror stories is the only rational way of dealing with corporate training sessions. It appeared in the British Fantasy Society's *Dark Horizons* in the winter 2011 issue.

'The Last Dance of Humphrey Bear': Humphrey Bear was a kids' TV character when I was growing up, and I've always found men in animal suits to be vaguely sinister. It was written at the height of the Victoria Climbie scandal when my girls were little, so there's a fair dollop of very personal outrage in it, and appeared in *Dark Horizons* in Summer 2011.

'How to Get Ahead in Avatising': Gods and goddesses don't come from heaven - they're made, by modern PR companies manipulating the archetypes of the collective unconscious. The problem is that once you've incarnated a deity in a human body, it's a little hard to control them. This was written for *The Alchemy Press Book of Urban Mythic 2*.

'Junk Male': As with all the best urban legends, this has a grain of truth in it. When I was a *styoodent* I shared a house with three other post-grads and we actually did create fake personae with which to reply to all the junk mail we got. To this day I still have a Lufthansa frequent flyer card in the name of Hildegard von Sputnik. This appeared in the charity anthology *Den of Eek 2: Urban Legends*, which you should also buy.

'The Decorative Water Feature of Nameless Dread': HP Lovecraft meets Tony Hancock with a dash of John Wyndham and *Gardeners' Question Time* thrown in. Suburban man discovers that a Deep One has made its home in his fish pond, and his shubunkins are not happy. It surfaced in 01Publishing's *Whispers from the Abyss*, in October 2013.

'The Gestalt Princess': The brief for this was a 'steampunk fairy tale', and it appeared in Sky Warrior Books' *Gears and Levers* Volume one in 2012.

'The Smith of Hockley': This blended a lot of random bits and pieces that had been kicking around in my head for a while: the discovery of the Staffordshire Hoard, the destruction of the Longbridge car factory and the impoverishment of the communities that relied on it. Birmingham was once known as 'the toyshop of Europe' because of the massive variety of consumer goods manufactured there – if the legendary Wayland Smith was going to be living anywhere in modern Britain, it would have to be the Jewellery Quarter. Published in *The Alchemy Press Book of Urban Mythic*, September 2013.

'If Street': This was an attempt to write a proper grown-up story about Issues. Not that it's autobiographical at all, but when I was in primary school I did inexplicably find myself mates with the school bad boy due to a shared passion for *Doctor Who*, and I'm not sure which of us was more surprised. I always wonder how his life turned out. This story appeared in *The Alchemy Press Book of Ancient Wonders* in 2012.

'Mob Rule': A failed submission to an anthology about astrological signs, which I'm very pleased to see out in the open at last, because how often do you get to write a story about a lecherous were-goat? This is its first appearance in print.

'The Gas Street Octopus': This was my first stab at a story for *Den of Eek 2: Urban Legends*, which they couldn't use because apparently they had a run on stories about octopuses. Who knew? To be fair, they were all better than mine. It appeared as a freebie on my blog, but this is its first appearance in print too.

'DIYary of the Dead': Just an excuse for a horrible pun, really. This will also appear in Knightwatch Press' *Pun Book of Horror*, but is reproduced here by kind permission of Theresa Derwin.

'The Curzon Street Horror': There is a disused railway terminus at Curzon Street in Birmingham which is the mirror image of the original terminus of Euston Street Station, all that remains of a doomed attempt by Victorian occultists to travel faster than steam through dimensions which no human was meant to see. A mummified cat holds the key – quite literally, in fact. The cat used to be in a display box in the old station building, but it's since gone into storage while HS2 is being built. One can only hope it makes a reappearance in the new development, because what says 'welcome to our city' better than a dead cat? Published in Fringeworks' *Weird Trails* in 2013.

'The Remover of Obstacles': This is a homage to all the trashy horror paperbacks of my Mum's that I used to read as a kid – and in particular a gem of a tale from Christopher Fowler called 'Last Call for Passenger Paul', which does it so much better. One of the few stories that I actually sat down and consciously planned, which is ironic because it then remained in limbo for years until it was picked up by Anachron Press and published in *Urban Occult* in 2013.

'Made From Locally Sourced Ingredients': This is a *Narrows* tale, in that it inhabits the same world as my first novel, *The Narrows*. Posh dining terrifies me, basically. Published in Knightwatch Press' *The Last Diner*, in September 2014.

'The Pigeon Bride': This is the last story here because it was first story I ever had published (not counting the one I wrote when I was eight that my Gran got printed in her local paper). It won a short story competition run by the Midlands edition of *The Big Issue* in 2002 to write a 'modern Midlands fable'. The judges described it as a 'credible synthesis of (their) themes with an unforeseen ending that was difficult to get right and a dark theme to sustain it.' I just thought it was an cool idea to make a pigeon the hero for a change.

James Brogden

Published by The Alchemy Press

www.alchemypress.co.uk

FROM THE ALCHEMY PRESS

Leinster Gardens and Other Subtleties

The ghost stories of Jan Edwards.

Fourteen short stories from Jan Edwards, including the BFS award short-listed 'Otterburn', plus a previously unpublished tale.

Concerning Events at Leinster Gardens: *He handed the maid his hat and replaced it with a coronet of silk holly leaves and tinsel. She gave him only the smallest raise of an eyebrow. 'Ghost of Christmas Present,' he said…*

The Waiting: *She picked up the hem of her night-dress and ran the length of the gallery. She wanted to race them to the door, to greet her father. Why, then, did a tiny part of her hesitate? Why should she be afraid? From the landing she heard the doors of the great hall being flung open…*

The Ballad of Lucy Lightfoot: *This had been in the planning for a very long time, for centuries – to the where and the when that the Wite had sent her. Across an entire continent to the edges of the Ottoman lands, to a place and time long before the Lightfoot name had ever begun. Her children, and her children's children, for more generations than she could count, were dust. Only she remained.*

From the introduction: …Ghost stories. Adeptly told, often with a sense of locale and time neatly placed within the narratives. Her family history informs and inspires some of her stories. Folklore figures as a focus in more than one story, whether urban myth or historical lore. But ghostly they are and deceptively disturbing.

Lightning Source UK Ltd.
Milton Keynes UK
UKOW04f1912171215

264964UK00001B/37/P